The Mojito Coast

This Large Print Book carries the Seal of Approval of N.A.V.H.

The Mojito Coast

Richard Helms

THORNDIKE PRESS
A part of Gale, Cengage Learning

Detroit • New York • San Francisco • New Haven, Conn • Waterville, Maine • London

Thorndike Press, a part of Gale, Cengage Learning.

Thorndike Press® Large Print Mystery.
The text of this Large Print edition is unabridged.
Other aspects of the book may vary from the original edition.
Set in 16 pt. Plantin.

LIBRARY OF CONGRESS CATALOGING-IN-PUBLICATION DATA

Helms, Richard W., 1955–
The mojito coast / by Richard Helms. — Large print edition.
pages ; cm. — (Thorndike Press large print mystery)
ISBN 978-1-4104-6307-4 (hardcover) — ISBN 1-4104-6307-9 (hardcover) 1. Military—Fiction. 2. Havana (Cuba)—History—20th century—Fiction. 3. Large type books. I. Title.
PS3608.E466M65 2013b
813'.6—dc23 2013025555

Published in 2013 by arrangement with Richard Helms

Printed in the United States of America
1 2 3 4 5 6 7 17 16 15 14 13

For Robert B. Parker
Thanks for making the
violent hero a bit more human.

Chapter One

Every time I flew into Cuba, I dreaded I might have to shoot my way out.

I hoped this time would be different, as I shifted my weight from foot to foot, waiting for the José Martí Airport customs agent to finish examining my passport.

At length, he placed it down on the table in front of him.

"Purpose of visit?" he asked.

"Business."

"What is your business in Cuba?"

I debated how to answer. For once, I wasn't entering the country for nefarious purposes. I supposed the truth would do.

"I'm a private investigator. A man in Miami sent me to find his fourteen-year-old daughter, and bring her back home."

His eyes narrowed as he scanned me again from head to toe. From his perspective, I think I suddenly seemed a lot more dangerous. From my perspective, so did he.

"You have firearms?"

"A pistol. It's in my suitcase, broken down."

He jerked my gator-hide valise off the floor and plopped it down on the table. Using both hands at once, he snapped the locks and pulled it open gingerly, as if he expected my midget accomplice to spring out at him. It took him about ten seconds to find the Colt .38 automatic I had stowed in the side pocket, broken down after I finished cleaning it before getting on the plane in Miami.

He laid the pieces on the tabletop, and examined them. He seemed interested in the serial number.

Finally, he looked at me.

"You plan to shoot someone in Havana?"

"Like I said, I'm here to find a girl and take her back to Miami. The gun is for self-defense. I always take it with me when I travel abroad. If I meant to kill someone, I'd have kept it on me in a holster."

And, I could have added, if I had meant to kill someone, I probably would have started with *him.*

"I will write down the serial number of this gun," he said, jotting in his notebook. "We will look for you when you leave, Señor Loame. I would be upset if the gun is not with you then."

I understood his concern. While stateside I had followed the unrest in Cuba in the papers. The Cuban dictator, Fulgencio Batista, was in real trouble, harried constantly by a band of commie outlaws holed up in the mountains outside Havana. There was talk of an insurrection. The United States had placed an embargo on the importation of weapons.

The customs guy was worried my gun might be sold to the Communists. It was a reasonable concern. In a country where weapons were at a premium and a decent dinner out could cost the average Cuban two weeks' pay, I could probably get a hundred for it easily. Maybe more.

It took a few moments, then he seemed satisfied that I posed little risk, and he cleared my entrance into the country with a flurry of stamping my passport.

"And where will you be staying in Havana?" he asked.

"The Riviera. I have reservations."

"Very good, señor. Please enjoy your stay in Cuba."

I retrieved my belongings and made my way through the airport to the parking lot. I hailed a taxi and told the driver to take me to the Riviera.

Even compared to Miami, Havana was roasting. The wind had shifted, coming off the Caribbean instead of from the mountains, and in the time it took to grab the cab my shirt was soaked through.

The drive from the airport to downtown Havana was both exhilarating and depressing. Like most of the Caribbean, Cuba bustled with capitalist enterprises while remaining as cash-poor as an itinerant Midwest tent preacher. The people, mostly Negroes with a smattering of Amerinds and people of no particular discernible extraction, seemed happy enough on first glance. I didn't have to look much deeper, though, to see the busy desperation in their movement around the city.

Starvation was never more than one missed meal away for the residents of this island republic, and Batista had a tight fist around the economy. That was probably why I had such an easy time passing through the customs office armed. Any *yanqui,* even one with a gun, was welcome, especially if he was staying at Lansky's new Riviera Hotel. The US dollars coming in outweighed any possible mayhem I might commit before going back home.

The driver stopped in the circular drive in front of the Riviera, and helped me take my bag up to the bellman at the door. He got a quarter for his trouble, which was probably as much as he would make in tips the rest of the day. I carried my own bag past the disappointed bellman and headed straight for the front desk.

"Cormac Loame," I told the registration clerk. "I made a reservation by telegram yesterday."

"Yes, Señor Loame," the clerk said, beaming at me. "We have been expecting you. If you would please sign here . . ."

The clerk started to hand me my key. A bony brown hand snaked in and grabbed it away from him. I turned toward a familiar face.

"Mac," said Lieutenant Jaime Guzman, of the Havana police, "so nice to have you visiting again. May I escort you to your room?"

The way he placed his hand on my arm made it clear the request had been only a pretense at friendship. He walked me to the elevators.

"Let me guess," I said. "The customs agent at the airport called you."

"He called the department," Guzman said. "The word eventually got around to me. Imagine my concern when I found you were back in Cuba. And with a gun, no less."

In retrospect, I probably should have advised Jaime that I was on the way to Havana. If anyone in Cuba had a right to know I was coming, he did. I had been in Cuba three times over the previous ten years. On two of those visits, Jaime had placed me on a plane headed back to the States, usually with an armed guard. I'd always left one or two bodies in my wake.

It was as I had told the customs agent — I needed the gun for self-defense. Cuba was a dangerous country in the mid-1950s, filled with twentieth-century versions of the old buccaneers. A man could become wealthy in the right business there, but he could also disappear without a trace. I involved myself in the business of dangerous people, and often they tried to make me go away. When I didn't discourage easily, they tried to make me die.

I don't die easily, either.

"I understand you are looking for a girl," Jaime said.

"Fourteen years old. She came here, according to her father, with an older man. The father wants her back. He can't come to Cuba, so he sent me."

"What is her name? Perhaps I can help."

By which, of course, he meant he could speed me on my way back to Miami before

I started littering the landscape with corpses again. Jaime is purposefully transparent, not stupid. He knew I understood him. He liked it when we communicated directly. It would have been impolite of him, though, to hand me my hat and ask why I was in a hurry.

We reached my room, on the fourth floor, and he made a point of opening the door for me. I pushed past him and tossed my valise on the rack next to the bathroom. At one time in Havana it was not always automatic to have a private bath in your hotel room. Lansky had seen to it that his hotel had all the modern conveniences expected by well-heeled American libertines visiting the island, from modern showers to central air-conditioning. I was spending Cecil Hacker's money, and I had decided to make myself comfortable.

I fished a photograph from my jacket pocket, and handed it to Jaime.

"Her name's Lila Hacker," I said. "Fourteen, white, blonde and blue. About five feet six. Keep it. I have more."

He stared at the picture of a girl who looked like a young Veronica Lake.

"This girl is fourteen years old?"

"Yeah, it's scary," I said. "You wouldn't guess it to look at her. The guy who brought her here worked for her father. He knows her true age, so he has no excuse."

"His name?"

"Danny McCarl."

"Have you a photograph of him?"

"No. We couldn't seem to find one before I left. Mr. Hacker's going to send one along via wirephoto shortly."

"And what will you do if you find Mr. McCarl and this Lila Hacker?"

"That's easy. I take Lila back to Miami."

"And Mr. McCarl?"

"I wasn't told to take him anywhere. He can stay here, for all I care."

"He will let the girl go? Just like that?"

I pulled off my lightweight linen jacket and tossed it on the bed. I turned back to Jaime and shrugged.

"Maybe he will. Maybe he won't. I don't care. When I find the girl, she's going back home."

Jaime took a seat in one of the Naugahyde chairs next to the window and pulled a thin cigar out of his jacket pocket. He made a show of lighting it and then let the smoke fall about his face like a laurel. He shook his head as the smoke dissipated.

"This will end badly, I think."

"I don't intend it that way. I might have to rough up McCarl a little, if he gives me any trouble, but I wasn't told to kill him."

He fingered the photo of Lila Hacker.

"I will keep this, since you don't mind. The next time you contemplate a visit to Havana, Mac, I'd appreciate it if you'd let me know before you get on the airplane. It was embarrassing to find out you were here from a lowly customs agent."

He rose from the seat and extended his hand. I grasped it. Once again, it seemed that we understood each other.

He started to leave, but stopped at the door.

"I have to ask this. This girl? She is the only reason you are in Cuba?"

"What do you mean?"

"I think you know."

I leaned against the cypress dresser, and stuffed my hands in my pants pockets.

"Is she still around?"

He scowled and grasped the doorknob as if he wanted to be about anywhere else.

"I don't think she needs to see you. Things have changed since you were here last. Marisol is married."

Something like a cold cascade of water flowed down the inside of my chest. I had suspected this, but she hadn't bothered to tell me.

"Who did she marry?"

"Hector Gonzalez."

Shit!

"Hell, Jaime, there must be about a million Hector Gonzalezes in Cuba. You want to narrow the field for me?"

He took another puff on the cigar and exhaled slowly.

"It's *that* Hector Gonzalez. She seems happy, Mac. Hector, though, is not going to be happy to discover you in the country. If you see Marisol, he will find out about it. Do everyone a favor. Let her go."

I ran one hand over my blond crew cut.

"It would be nice if I could."

There was nothing he could say to that, so he pulled the door closed as he left.

I was suddenly tired. I switched on the radio, pulled off my trousers and shirt, and dropped down onto the bed. I stared at the ceiling for a long time, trying to sort out all the lumber in my thick Irish skull.

Chapter Two

Two days earlier, I had been sitting at my desk on the fifth floor of the Chase Bank Building on Biscayne Boulevard in Miami. Christmas was less than a week away, but even so it was a steamy day, with white billowy clouds hanging over the ocean, waiting for an opportunity to coalesce and pull together the energy to let loose with an afternoon thunderstorm. I would have welcomed it. It would have broken up the monotony.

I was finishing a report on my most recent case, an insurance fraud. It was routine. I probably could have handed to my secretary any other fraud report I'd ever written and instructed her to write in the offender's name, but that would have been cheating. The oscillating fan sitting on a table next to the desk threatened to scatter my work every ten seconds. My plans were to finish the report, send it to the client and then take a few days off to lie on the beach and avoid the holiday as much as I possibly could. When there's nobody in your life who matters, things like Christmas don't count for much.

Next to the report was another distraction. I had visited a new car dealer that morning to look at the latest Buick Roadmaster. It had been redesigned for 1958, and I had allowed myself to be talked into taking a test ride. All I had taken away from the dealer was a brochure, but I had been looking at it all day, trying to figure out where I was going to come up with two grand.

At a little after three, the secretary I shared with an insurance salesman and a chiropractor knocked on my door. I wasn't aware of any appointments scheduled for that day. In fact, I didn't have any on the schedule for the rest of the week. Nobody wanted to find divorce papers in their Christmas stockings. It was doldrums season in the detective biz.

The secretary showed a gentleman in. He wore a month of my income on his body. The price of his Italian shoes alone could have fed me for a week, and I have a healthy appetite. He was in his early fifties, with hair going gray at the temples, thinning at the crown. His ears were gnarled, like dried fungus. A scar like a thin knotted cord under his skin ran diagonally from his left eyebrow back into his hairline. He looked as though he'd been a boxer earlier in his life, and not a good one, judging by the permanent swollen tissue over his eyes and around his nose. Whatever career decision he might have made after fighting had obviously been a good one.

It took me a moment, but then I knew exactly who he was.

"Please, Mr. Hacker, have a seat," I said. I pulled a box of Havanas from my desk drawer, and opened it. "Would you like a cigar?"

"You know me?" he asked.

"I saw you fight the Bomber in nineteen forty-one, Chicago."

"You got a good memory."

"It was a short fight."

"A smart mouth, too. I'll take one of those cigars."

I handed him one and slid a lighter across the desk. He bit the end of the cigar and spat it into my wastebasket. He took a couple of puffs and waved his hand in the air, like a giant Virginia ham attached to five knockwursts.

"We should get down to business," he

said. "I need you to go to Cuba."

I had considered having a cigar myself, but this sidetracked me. I'm sure I must have grimaced.

"I don't much like Cuba," I said.

He pulled a picture from his inside jacket pocket, and leaned forward to hand it to me.

"My daughter, Lila. I married her mother near the end of the war. We were together long enough to make a honeymoon at the Fontainebleau Hotel before I shipped out to Europe. Lila was born while I was overseas. By the time I got back . . . well, we're both men of the world, Mr. Loame. I'm sure you've gotten a *Dear John* letter or two in your time."

I had, but I didn't feel like talking about it.

"It took me months to track Lila's mother down. She lived in California, of all places. She had filed for divorce, was gonna marry some insurance salesman out in Palo Alto. I suppose it made sense. He was stable, dependable. I hadn't done nothing but fight all my life, first in the ring, then in the war. I was young, stupid and angry. I threatened to beat the hell out of the kid she was getting ready to divorce me for. Then I saw Lila, my daughter. Less than a year old and she was already a beauty. I left the house, hopped on the bus, and rode back here to Florida. Her mother died in fifty-four. The insurance salesman never adopted Lila. I refused to allow it. So she came to live with me."

"Excuse me, Mr. Hacker," I said. "What does this have to do with Cuba?"

"I got this guy who works for me, kind of a bodyguard. Danny McCarl. He was a third-rate punching bag in the ring, but that still makes him twice as good as most guys on the street. He started hanging out with Lila. I didn't like it, but she did, and you know how it is. I have a hard time refusing her."

"How old is this McCarl?"

"Twenty-six. Almost twice her age, Mr. Loame. Both Lila and McCarl disappeared about five days ago. I put out the word, and this morning I talked with a ticket agent at Pan Am. Seems they hopped a plane to Havana the day they went missing."

"You want me to go after them?"

"She's underage. He took her out of the country for carnal purposes."

"I hear your attorney talking there."

He smiled, displaying yellowing teeth that pointed in all sorts of directions.

"Yeah, I spoke with him already. He don't

think it would be much of a problem with the authorities if someone was to go down there and bring her back."

"And since McCarl isn't a Cuban citizen, nobody would be overly distraught if he didn't come with her."

"Or if he never came back at all."

"Mr. Hacker, who is your attorney?"

"I think you know him. Gerald Turnbloom."

I knew him, all right. The only time I'd killed anyone in the forty-eight, he'd represented me. He'd gotten me cleared after demonstrating to the court that it was me or the other guy and the other guy got off the first shot. It didn't hurt that the other guy was a well-known hard-ass who'd spent most of his adult life eating state food at Raiford. Counting on Gerry Turnbloom's humanity was a sucker bet at best, but if you were facing the prospect of twenty years eating state food, he was the guy you wanted in your corner.

"Sir, I don't know what it is you're looking for, exactly. If I do this, though, you need to understand something. I might go down to Cuba, and I might bring back your daughter. Anything else that happens is unplanned. I'm not going down there as your hired gun. McCarl doesn't give me any trouble, I plan to keep it nice and quiet."

He shrugged, held out his hands and said, "I wouldn't have it any other way."

"So, why don't you go down there yourself?" I asked. "It's not like you don't have enough money and you have plenty of tough guys working for you. Why'd you decide to come to me?"

"I got some legal problems coming up," he said. "It ain't been in the papers yet, but the Feds are unhappy with the way I been doing my books. They plan to make some tax trouble for me in the next couple of weeks. It will hit the papers tomorrow or the next day. Better if I don't leave the country, you know what I mean?"

I thought it would be better if *I* didn't leave the country, either. On the other hand, it was the doldrums season and the Roadmaster had been a sweet-riding car.

"Job will go two grand and expenses," I said.

"That's a lot."

"Anytime I have to go out of the country, the price goes up," I said. "Even more if I have to go to Cuba. They don't like me much down there."

He reached into his jacket pocket, pulled out a fat calfskin wallet, and dropped a wad of bills on my desk. I was always quick with numbers. There was almost three thousand dollars there.

"You need more expense money, you wire my office here in Miami," he said.

I nodded and asked if he wanted a receipt.

"Naw. Turnbloom says you're straight, Mr. Loame. I reckon you ain't gonna stiff me or nothing. Would be bad for business, right?"

I imagined it would. Stiffing Cecil "The Madman" Hacker probably wouldn't do my health any wonders, either.

"You find my little girl and you bring her back home, okay?" he said. "I don't care what happens to McCarl, but you bring Lila back inside a week and maybe there'll be a bonus."

He turned and walked out without saying good-bye.

Chapter Three

So, I was back in Cuba.

Things had changed a little since my previous visit in 1952. Batista, with a little financial help from American mobsters, had run Socorros off the island right after I had made my last mad dash back to Miami. With Socorros out of the picture, Batista had put out the welcome mat to every low-life and ne'er-do-well on the planet, but he had a particular affinity for the gangsters who had brought him back to power. The mobs had moved in with a passion. Traffi-cante had built the Sans Souci. Meyer Lan-sky countered it with the Riviera, where I was staying. Gambling and whoring were almost as popular as baseball and jai alai. Batista took his action right off the top.

Marisol was married to Hector Gonzalez. That was one change I hadn't anticipated.

The order of the day, however, was find-ing Lila Hacker. As soon as I did, I could point my backside at this island paradise and get back to my digs in Miami.

I had given it a little thought on the short airplane trip across the water. Danny McCarl had to know that if he took Lila, there would be repercussions. Cecil Hacker was an ex-boxer, but he wasn't an idiot. In the years after the Second World War, he had aligned himself with Sam Giancana in Chicago, who had hooked him in with Santo Trafficante in Miami. Although Hacker, being Irish, would never be a made man, he had talents Trafficante found useful. Hacker ran four or five businesses in South Florida that were known fronts for money laundering.

I had come into contact with Trafficante's operation myself once or twice. In general, I tried to keep a lot of real estate between me and the mobs. In a place like Miami, though — or Brooklyn or Chicago or Vegas, or damned near any populated area nowadays — sometimes it seemed like you couldn't wipe your sweat without dribbling a little on a wiseguy.

So, I surmised, if Danny McCarl had spirited Lila Hacker away to the land of rum and rumba, he must have thought he would be protected in some way should Hacker ask Trafficante for help in getting her back.

In Havana, protection under the Batista regime usually meant other mobs. What I didn't know was whether that meant rival American gangs or one of the homegrown sugar syndicates.

After a bath and a shave, I dressed in a pair of summer wool trousers, a cotton shirt and a light jacket that barely concealed the .38 in my shoulder holster. With rebels infesting the mountains outside Havana, a lot of guys walked around town with side-arms. Even so, I didn't want to draw attention as an armed *gringo.*

It had been six long years since my last trip to Cuba. Things change. I hoped I could still scare up some of my old snitches.

My first stop was a shop on Compostela. The sign in front hadn't changed. I stepped inside.

A woman behind the counter asked if she could help me.

"I'm looking for Escobar," I said, in my out-of-practice Spanish.

"Which Escobar? The old one or the young one?"

I had never known that Escobar had a son.

"The old one."

"Not here. Not for a long time."

"You know where I can locate him?"

"You ask young Escobar."

Before I could stop her, she turned and disappeared behind a curtain separating the front counter from the back storeroom. I stood at the counter and waited. After a couple of minutes, she returned with a young man.

He looked a year or so on either side of twenty. His hair was coal black and combed back from his forehead. Without even looking I knew he would have a ducktail. Cuban kids liked to imitate the stuff they saw in American movies. Probably thought it made him look tough. He was wrong.

He wore tan gabardine pants and a dark shirt unbuttoned halfway to his chest, over which he had put on a white linen jacket. That was about as dressed up as most Cuban kids ever got.

"Yes?" he asked. "I am Escobar."

"I was looking for your father, the older Escobar."

"Why are you looking for him?"

I handed the kid one of my cards and hoped he could read English.

"I'm from Miami. Escobar helped me in the past with information."

The kid stared at the card for a moment. I could see his lips move as he worked his way over the words, and I recalled that — under Batista — education had pretty much gone to the dogs.

"You pay for this information?" Escobar said, in halting English.

"If it's good."

"Maybe I give you information."

"Maybe I need to talk with your father."

He pulled his jacket away, so I could see the knife parked in his belt.

I pulled my jacket aside and patted my .38.

"Look, kid," I said. "Just tell me where I can find Escobar."

The kid seemed to shrink inside his clothes.

"At home," he said. "He's not well. Very sick."

"I'm sorry to hear it. You want to take me to see him?"

The boy nodded and walked past me through the door.

I followed him out onto Compostela. The heat and humidity slapped me like a giant palm. Christmas in less than a week and it felt like July. You had to love the tropics.

The kid led me up Compostela to Lamparilla and cut a right toward the water. I kept him three feet in front of me. I didn't want him to get any heroic ideas. It was too damned hot to kill anyone. If I plugged the kid for making a run at me, old Escobar probably wouldn't tell me anything I wanted to know.

After a block or so, young Escobar pointed at a dilapidated frame house. "Inside," he said.

"Lead the way."

He took me through the central door and up a flight of creaky stairs to an apartment on the second floor. Without knocking, he opened the door.

"Papa!" he called out. "There is an American here to see you."

He crooked his finger, gesturing for me to follow him. I pulled the Colt from my shoulder holster and held it steady against my right thigh. For all I knew the kid was leading me into a room full of Cubano teenaged thugs.

I wasn't going to fall for that one.

Not again.

If young Escobar noticed the gun, he didn't show it. He opened a door, and held it for me. Though the doorway I could see a frail figure lying on a narrow bed. From ten feet away, it was hard to tell whether this was Escobar. A smell like rancid fruit swept through the door and enveloped me. I fought the urge to gag.

"Escobar," I said. "It's Loame."

The head on the pillow rotated in my

direction.

"Padrè?" he said. His voice was not much more than a raspy whisper.

I stepped closer. The face was drawn and tight against the skull and I could see the map of blue veins through his translucent skin, but the eyes belonged to Escobar. I pulled a rickety wooden chair up to the bed.

"It's Cormac Loame," I said. "From Miami."

Escobar's eyes were dimly focused on some space far, far away.

"Will you hear my confession?" he asked.

I turned to the kid. He shrugged.

"Been like that for two, three weeks. Maybe gonna die, but he don't seem to be in a hurry."

"He needs a doctor."

"The doctor's come," the kid said. "Three, four days ago. Gave him pills, said was all he could do, said it's a matter of time."

"He doesn't recognize me," I said. "He thinks I'm a priest."

"He don't know anyone. Everyone is priest to him. I think he has lotsa things to get off his chest."

"You knew he wouldn't be able to help me. Why the hell did you bring me here?"

"You had gun. You not want to hear what I had to say. You want to see the old man.

So I bring you here."

I couldn't take my eyes off the paper-thin skin stretched like a drum over Escobar's angular skull.

"A man brought a young girl from Florida several days ago," I said. "The girl is only fourteen. I know that doesn't mean much here, but it's against the law in Miami. I need to find the man and the girl so I can take her back."

"When you find, you kill this man?"

"Not if I don't have to. One way or the other, though, the girl goes home."

The kid nodded.

"I don't know nothing about your man and girl. The old man, he have a friend named Luis Gopaldo. They'd spend lotsa time together. Maybe Luis help you."

"Where can I find Luis?"

"At El Floridita, on Obispo near Monserrate. You know the place?"

"I know it. What's he look like?"

"He's big, fat, sweats all the time. You can't miss him."

"Padrè?" Escobar pleaded again as I started to back away from the bed.

"For God's sake," I said to the kid, "get a damned priest up here."

Chapter Four

El Floridita was a squat, pinkish building set in among multistory business palaces on Obispo near the Ambos Mundos Hotel, in Habana Vieja, the old part of town. Cigarette smoke rolled out the door as I opened it. Inside, it was pleasantly dim and cool, compared with the razor sunlight and searing heat on the sidewalk.

I scanned the room, looking for anyone who fit young Escobar's description of Luis Gopaldo. Nobody stood out. I crossed the room to the mahogany bar. Behind it was an ancient mural of a waterfront scene instead of the typical mirror. A lot of people came to Havana to get away from everything. They sure didn't want to watch their reflections as they sought refuge from themselves in the bottom of a highball glass.

As soon as I took a seat, a young man appeared in front of me.

"Good afternoon, señor!" he said. "What

is your pleasure?"

"Something cold and wet."

"Would you like to try a mojito?"

"What in hell is a mojito?"

"The mojito," said a man several stools away, "is the best drink there is. A fine drink. A strong drink."

He was bearish, in faded khaki shorts and a worn madras shirt with rolled sleeves. The shirt was unbuttoned and his barrel torso spilled out from it. The pants were secured to his protruding waist by a belt with a massive metal buckle that read *Gott Mit Uns.* His voice slurred, but his eyes riveted on me like fifty-caliber gun sights.

"You want a mojito," he said, his high, halting voice betraying his robust body. There was an accent there, like Gary Cooper, only more colloquial. It was a voice one didn't expect to hear in Havana. It was the kind of voice you hear from expats in bars all over the world.

"Sir?" the bartender said.

"I guess I want a mojito," I said.

"Good choice," the bear several stools down said. "It's a simple thing, really. Much better than the plebeian daiquiri. My God, you're a big one. Come over as freight, did you?"

I tried to ignore him, but he drew himself

from his stool by grasping the bar and pulling. There was an exhalation of air from his mouth, a sort of *oof,* and he was on his feet. He shambled down to the stool next to me and settled onto it. I could smell half a day of drinking through the jungle of whitening whiskers on his face. He drew the bartender's attention by coughing and waving his hand, then gave the man some kind of signal. The bartender nodded.

"Watch him," the man said. "The secret to the mojito is the man who makes it."

I watched the bartender, if only to avoid looking at the wreck sitting next to me. I made a silent vow that, should I ever come to his state, I'd take a couple of strong drinks and muffle the loud end of a shotgun with my mouth.

The bartender set the drink in front of me. It looked much like a daiquiri, which immediately set me against it. I took a sip. It was like drinking a candy cane.

I crooked a finger at the bartender and took out my gun. I slid it onto the bar, taking care not to place it in a pool of water. I waited until he was in front of me. "Look at me," I said.

"Yes, sir?"

"Do you think you would remember my face?"

He probably wouldn't because he couldn't take his eyes off the gun.

"Yes, sir," he said.

"Good. Now, I would like to make this perfectly clear. Should you ever see this face in your bar again, do not — repeat — do *not* offer me a mojito. Do we understand each other?"

"Yes, sir, we understand each other clearly."

I placed the gun back in my holster.

"Good. Now, get me a beer."

"What brand, sir?"

"*Any* brand!"

The bartender quickly removed himself to the taps. The man sitting next to me nodded.

"Damned fine," he said. "Agree with you in every respect. Beer's much better. I gotta go take a piss."

He pulled himself from the stool again, and lumbered toward the back of the room.

When the bartender returned with a schooner of beer, I placed several bills on the bar.

"I need to talk with Luis Gopaldo," I said.

"I have not seen him all day."

"When does he usually come in?"

He shrugged and started to clean a glass. Probably the first time he'd done it all day.

I placed two more bills on the bar. He pretended not to notice, but I saw him glance at them out of the corner of his eye.

I took one bill back.

That got his attention.

"Every time I have to repeat a question, another one disappears. Luis Gopaldo."

"He was in early this morning. He usually comes in for a drink around *seis.*"

I checked my watch. It was five-thirty. Even in the tropics the sun is pretty low by that time in December.

The bear shambled out of the bathroom and made his way back to the bar. He slapped the mahogany with one bloated hand. It made a thudding sound.

"Gonna go fishing," he said. He turned to me. "Wanna go fishing?"

"Not today."

"I gotta nice boat. Wanna see my boat?"

"No," I said, without taking my eyes off the bartender.

"It's a good boat, a strong boat. A fisherman's boat. You oughta see it."

"Some other time," I said. "I'm waiting for someone."

"Suit yourself. Going fishing."

He shuffled out of the bar.

"See you tomorrow, sir!" the bartender called.

The man didn't look back. He raised his arm, gave a backhanded salute, and kept stumbling into the dusk.

"Here's what's going to happen," I said. "You get to keep this money. In return, when Gopaldo comes in, you point him out to me. I'll be at the table over in the corner. You understand?"

He nodded. I held out my schooner. He refilled it and I retreated to the darkness of my corner table.

Chapter Five

I had wasted my money on the bartender. I picked Gopaldo out the minute he walked into El Floridita about a half hour later. He looked exactly the way Escobar's kid had described him. The bartender nodded at him and then looked directly at me. I gave him an OK sign.

Gopaldo started to settle in at the bar. Something, though, passed between him and the bartender. With some effort, Gopaldo pivoted toward me. He tried to make me out in the dim light of the corner. Then he turned back to the bar and shrugged. The bartender brought him a beer.

Gopaldo took a sip of the beer, then walked across the bar to my table. Without being invited, he slid a chair out and collapsed into it.

"I am Luis Gopaldo."

"I know."

"I do not know you."

"Escobar knows me."
"Escobar is dead."
"Not quite yet."
"As good as dead. Escobar does not know who he is or who anyone else is. In a day or two . . ." He shrugged again.
"His kid told me where to find you."
"The young one," Gopaldo said and feigned spitting on the floor. "He needs to learn when to keep his mouth shut. What do you want?"
I slowly and carefully took one of my cards from my inside jacket pocket. I knew the second Gopaldo walked into the room that he wore a fancy shoulder rig and there was no reason to wear one unless you needed it to carry something lethal. I didn't want him to get the wrong idea.
I slid the card across the table to him. He picked it up.
"You are Loame?"
I nodded.
"Escobar told me about you."
"What did he say?"
"That you are unlucky for other people."
There was nothing to say to that, since it was more or less true.
At least in Cuba.
"Escobar used to provide me with information," I said. "We had an arrangement. I

was hoping you and I could come to an arrangement."

Gopaldo scratched his belly and took a sip of his beer.

"You want me to provide you with information?"

"If you can. I can pay for it."

"What you pay?"

"Let's try this. I'll tell you what I want to know and you tell me what you think it's worth."

"And if you don't think it's worth this?"

"We either negotiate or I hit the pavement."

"Just like that."

"There are lots of people in Havana who would be willing to tell me what I want to know. People in this city are desperate. A lot of them need money to get off the island."

"Get off? For what?"

"For Florida. We know all about the rebels. It's made the news in South Florida. The word is Batista already has his bags packed and an airplane on standby at the airport twenty-four hours a day."

"People tell tales," Gopaldo said. "This is Cuba, Loame. New governments are a way of life. What makes you think anything would change if these rebels kicked Batista out?"

"They're reds. You wouldn't like the way they run things."

"Even reds need things I can provide."

"Perhaps. About a week ago, a man entered Havana by way of the airport. He had a girl with him." I handed Gopaldo a copy of Lila's picture. "That girl."

He took a quick look at the picture and set it on the table.

"The girl is fourteen," I continued. "She's still a child. The man worked for Cecil Hacker. Hacker works for Santo Trafficante. I know Trafficante is here in Havana, which means the man who brought that girl here knew he would be protected. I would like to know who's protecting him."

"And I would like to be able to tell you, because information like that would cost you a lot of money. Unfortunately, I don't know."

"Can you find out?"

"I can ask questions — quietly, you understand."

"It goes without saying."

"That would mean I am working for you here in Havana, Mr. Loame?"

"You could see it that way."

"Sort of like your agent in Cuba."

"If you like."

"The kind of people I ask for information are going to want to be paid for it."

I peeled six or seven bills from my money clip. "You run out of that, you can find me through the concierge at the Riviera."

He folded the bills and tucked them into his jacket pocket. Then he pushed his chair back and stood. "I could take your money and not ask questions. I could tell you nobody had anything to tell me."

"You could also recall what your friend Escobar told you."

"That you are unlucky for other people?"

"Yes," I said.

Chapter Six

I grabbed a taxi back to the Riviera. It was almost dark, which was the time in Havana when the evening revelers came out to play. On the way to the hotel I noted the signs on the hotels and casinos. Tony Bennett was playing the Red Room, Dorothy Dandridge headlining at the Sans Souci.

The contrast between the trendy night-spots and places like the Shanghai, where the strippers wouldn't know a G-string from a flying saucer, was not lost on me. Havana was the banquet that would satisfy any desire — carnal or otherwise — you might bring in with you from the mainland. It didn't matter what you did on the island, when you went home your sins stayed behind. What happened in Havana tended to stay in Havana. Some advertising joker might take a notion like that and run with it, but that wasn't my game.

Meanwhile, I had watched news reports

earlier in the day on Havana's television station, CMQ, that the reds had taken Baire and San Luis.

A great time to party! I had to wonder, though, whether last call was around the corner.

Back at the Riviera, pictures of Tony Martin were plastered all over the lobby. He was the main attraction at the main stage in the Copa Room.

I checked in at the front desk to pick up my key.

"Mr. Loame," the clerk said. "I am so happy you came by. I have wonderful news. Mr. Smith has upgraded you!"

"Who is Mr. Smith, and why do I need upgrading?"

"Mr. Harry Smith, of course."

I looked at him the way a snake stares at a wheelbarrow.

"The hotel manager," the clerk explained.

"I see. And exactly how did Mr. Smith upgrade me?"

"We've moved you to a splendid tenth-floor corner room. You'll love it. It has a marvelous balcony overlooking the Malecòn."

The Malecòn is the main shore drive in Havana. It winds along the beach for several miles before terminating at the Calle del Prado.

"And how did I rate this upgrade?"

"I'm sure I have no idea. Please let me get your new room key for you. Your luggage and clothes have already been moved."

Which, of course, had afforded someone an opportunity to go through my things. I had never heard of Harry Smith and I had no idea why he might have wanted to move me into a swankier room. Somehow, I had a feeling someone more highly placed had put him up to it.

I took the key and the elevator to the tenth floor, and found my room quickly.

Compared to my original double-bed economy-class accommodations, the corner room was almost a palace. There was a king-size bed, and a television. My room on the fourth floor had a radio, but no TV. I liked the idea of having a TV all to myself in my hotel room. The bed was nice, too.

The clerk hadn't been kidding when he mentioned the view. I tossed my jacket on the dresser and draped my shoulder rig over the arm of the chair before taking a few minutes to survey the sights from my balcony. Across the Malecòn, I could see the running lights of fishing vessels and the occasional sailboat as they plied the inky night waters of the Caribbean. Romantic couples strolled along the seawall hand-in-hand, pausing now and then between streetlamps to grab a kiss or cuddle under the pregnant tropical moon.

I turned on the television, and cranked up the volume. Then I made a thorough search of my new digs. It didn't take long to find the microphone behind the headboard. I probably could have yanked it out of the wall, but then Mr. Harry Smith might decide to cancel my upgrade and I liked the new room.

I showered and checked out the news while I laid out my clothes for dinner. CMQ, based in Havana, gave me the best picture, but because it was the local channel and Havana was the capital, I had to presume the news had a decidedly pro-Batista slant.

Not surprisingly, the announcer claimed the rebels were being driven back from Baire. From the reports I had followed in Miami, I doubted it. So far, Cuba's military had enjoyed damned few successes against the reds.

Baire was some distance from Havana. I figured I had a week or so to find Lila Hacker before the country fell to the rebels, no matter how much sugar the CMQ announcer tried to scoop onto the political situation.

I dressed and headed for the casino.

Dinner was Argentine prime rib with a nice French red. People kept telling me that someday California was going to produce excellent wines, but I had my doubts. The beef was rare and tender and delicious with béarnaise sauce and horseradish on the side. The people seated around me were elegant. It was hard to imagine other people dying in swarms of gunfire in the jungles less than a hundred miles away.

After eating, I traded one of Cecil Hacker's hundreds for a stack of chips and took a seat at the first blackjack table I could find. Within seconds a pretty *chica* in a low-cut gown appeared at my side with a tray. I ordered a Manhattan.

Two drinks later and up forty bucks, I decided to quit while I was ahead. I had a feeling I was more or less at the end of my evening. It had been a long day, with the flight in, the hassles at the airport, and the issue of being in Havana at all. I strolled over to the bar and ordered a drink to take up to my room.

When I turned back around, I almost walked straight into Marisol Gonzalez.

She was lithe and warm, her milk-chocolate hair pulled back into a bun. I knew, from experience, that I only needed to pull two pins out and that hair would cascade across her bare shoulders. She wore a red halter cocktail dress with a neckline that plunged far enough to take my breath away. Her eyes were the same umber shade I remembered. Her lips glistened scarlet.

She still wore the same scent — *Ivoire.*

I think she was as shaken at our chance meeting as I was.

"Mac!" she exclaimed. "You . . . you're in Havana!"

Like most of the locals, she turned the *v* in the word into a *b,* as in *cabana.*

"Yes," I said, trying to think of something suave to say. It wasn't coming. "I'm on business. I didn't expect to run into you."

Her look told me she had never planned to see me again.

"A drink?" I asked.

She glanced around and then nodded. I took her arm and walked her over to a table, while gesturing for the waiter to take her order.

I cradled my Manhattan with both hands, the sweat on the glass cooling my palms. "I saw Jaime Guzman this morning," I said. "He told me about you and Hector."

She nodded again, her expression a little

panicky.

"I didn't know," I said. "Nobody sent me an invitation to the wedding or anything. I wouldn't have come, of course, but I'd have sent a gift. A toaster."

"Oh, Mac —"

"A waffle iron, maybe. Bottle of strychnine. You know — something useful."

She pushed her chair from the table and stood. "I have to go."

I grabbed her wrist — not strongly enough to frighten her, but enough to let her know I meant for her to stay. She stared at my hand clasped around her arm, and sat back down.

"I'm here on business. I didn't come to make trouble for you. Now that you're here, though, I want to look at you for a few minutes."

The waiter returned with a champagne cocktail for her. I paid him and he went away.

"You look good," I said. "I thought about you from time to time, up in Miami, and I imagined how you must look. Six years —"

"It was impossible. You are *Americano,* I am *Cubana.* It never would have worked. I could not leave my country. You can't live in Cuba. Your luck would last only so long here. Perhaps you have already run through all of it. I could not live with that, wondering each day whether you might not come home. It was better this way."

"Better? You think so? Why Hector? Of all the men in Cuba, you had to choose him?"

"It's been six years. Hector is an important man here. He is one of Fulgencio's trusted —"

She searched for the word.

"Accomplices?" I suggested.

I saw the color rise from that place just above her breasts that I knew so well, flaring across her neck and cheeks.

"If you can call a man like Batista by his first name, maybe I don't know you anymore after all," I said.

"No. You may not. Tell me, what is your life like now?"

I took a bracing sip of my drink and played a little with the ring of condensation on the table.

"I stay busy. I work. I live alone. I have a nice house. Once or twice a year I take a vacation to someplace where they've heard of snow. My work has paid well. I can afford a new car every several years. That's about it."

"Nobody . . . special?"

"I thought so. Now I guess I was imagining things."

Either she missed the inference or she ignored it.

"And your work, it has brought you to Havana?"

I pulled one of Lila Hacker's pictures from the breast pocket of my jacket and slid it across the table. "This girl is in Cuba. She was brought here by a man twice her age. Her father wants her back. Havana seemed the right place to look for her."

"Why?"

"Because the guy who brought her here is mixed up with mobsters. Havana is the last refuge in this country for the mob. The rebels —"

"Please," she said, placing a hand on mine, "don't talk about that. Not here."

"The mob? Or the rebels?"

"Both. You have been gone for a long time. You do not know how intertwined the government has become with criminal elements. Batista depends on his *Americano* business partners to help prop up the economy. They bring in guns. Did you know your country will no longer ship weapons or ammunition to Cuba, for fear it will wind up in the hands of the insurrectionists?"

"Now, how in hell is insurrectionists a better word than rebels?"

"Do not joke, Mac."

"Have you ever seen the Malecòn from a tenth-floor balcony at the Riviera?"

"Yes," she said.

"Want to see it again?"

"I fear that, in your present emotional state, you might throw me off of it."

A little bit of the tension dissipated. We both chuckled.

"No," I said. "Not you. Never you. Hector, maybe."

"I have to go."

"You don't. You might want to, but you don't *have* to. Six years, Marisol. Stay long enough for another drink."

"And then another? And one after that? Until you have rid me of all my inhibitions and I will accept your offer to view the Malecòn?"

"Isn't that what you want?"

For a moment I thought she was about to say yes.

Then she shook her head. "I could not bear it. Please, do not tempt me with things that are impossible. I have to go."

"Why are you here?"

"What?"

"You're a married woman. A married *Cuban* woman. By your own admission, your husband is an important man. Yet here you are, wandering around Meyer Lansky's casino as if you're trolling for something."

"You are insulting."

"I don't like coincidences. When I came back to the hotel this afternoon I had been moved to a luxury suite. I found a microphone there, behind my bed. That means someone knows I'm here and they want to know what I'm up to. Then, in what must be a divine coincidence, I run into you dolled up like a Cuban tart — and your loving husband nowhere to be seen. You should have told them I'm smarter than that."

"Please!" she begged, looking around.

"Don't worry. I won't make trouble. I probably wouldn't have taken you up to my room even if you'd agreed to go. Maybe I wanted to see how far you'd take it."

She fumbled with her clutch purse.

"Go on," I said. "The drink is paid for. There's nothing holding you here."

As if I'd pulled my gun on her, she walked away briskly, her stiletto heels clicking on the marble floors like ricocheting shrapnel.

I watched her disappear into the masses of people in the casino. I picked the picture of Lila Hacker off the table and slipped it into my pocket, where I felt the jumble of chips.

I was forty bucks to the good. I figured I might as well see if my run of luck really had run out.

I walked unsteadily toward the blackjack table, and settled, a bit too solidly, onto one of the seats. The waitress appeared again at my side. I liked the way they did that. I told her to bring me another Manhattan.

By the time she came back, I was down twenty bucks.

"Tell me something, sweetheart," I said, as I took the drink from her. "Have you ever seen the Malecòn from a tenth-floor balcony in this place?"

Chapter Seven

Her name was Élan, not Marisol, but her skin was the color of fine dark rum and her hair smelled like hyacinth as it flowed across my chest.

There was a sour taste in my mouth and a buzz between my ears. The morning sun cut into the room like a scythe.

I couldn't recall everything that had happened the night before, but she was naked and I was naked and the lingering aroma in the room told me we hadn't been talking politics.

She stirred slightly. Her hand stroked my chest. *"Bueno,"* she said. She slipped her hand down my stomach and under the sheet. Her eyes opened. *"Muy bueno!"*

"No," I said.

"What is it? Have I done something wrong?"

"No," I repeated. "I have. Thank you for last night."

She smiled at me and then stood and walked in bare everything into the bathroom. I heard the shower running. The drone of the water against the shower curtain and the song she hummed as she washed lulled me back to sleep.

I awoke when she sat on the bed next to me. She was dressed again in the hotel waitress outfit she had scattered about the room in our rush the night before.

"I must go," she said.

"Yes."

She held up a couple of fives. "I took the liberty."

"I was asleep. You could have taken it all."

"I am not a *puta,*" she said. "I took off early last night to come see the Malecòn from your balcony. I missed a great many tips. I did not think you would mind."

"No," I said. "Take it. Perhaps some other time."

She placed a finger on my lips.

"Do not trouble yourself, señor. Élan knows what is temporary, and what will last. I would not have come here with you if I had not wanted to."

She leaned over and kissed me lightly on the lips.

I showered and shaved and grabbed breakfast in the hotel restaurant. My head still buzzed from too much alcohol the night before and I didn't look forward to spending a whole day tramping around the city and shoving pictures of Lila Hacker under noses.

As I passed the front desk, the clerk caught my attention. "Señor Loame! I have a message for you."

Was it possible Gopaldo had found the girl that quickly?

Inside an envelope was a calling card that read *Federico Gonzalez* on the front. On the back was a message scribbled in English.

Heard you were in town, it read. *Come by for a visit. The Fronton Jai Alai. Rico.*

Hector Gonzalez may have detested me, but I had always gotten on well with his kid brother, Federico. A playboy, a rake and an overall cad, Rico Gonzalez was more invested in spending his family's considerable fortune than in expanding it. And, he had a passion for jai alai.

Havana's foremost venue, Fronton Jai Alai, was where Rico wanted to meet me.

The Fronton Jai Alai was managed by a man named Elicia Arguelles. The game is about as hard to explain as American football. The best way to describe it is to say it's like playing horse in mixed doubles squash on Benzedrine.

Eight teams play in each match, but only two are on the court, or *cancha,* at any given time. Each team has two players. All four players are on the same side of the court, with two in the frontcourt, and two in the backcourt, like in doubles squash. They wield curved wicker scoops called *cestas* that are attached to gloves and tied to their wrists with leather thongs. Once the ball is in play, it stays in play until someone misses it. The idea is to scoop the stony, goatskin-covered rubber ball — called a *pelota* — as it flies toward you from the wall, and then launch it back to the wall, and do it all in one movement without stopping.

The first team to score seven points wins, and a point may only last a minute or so, but that's fine because any longer than that and the players' hearts would explode. The winning team stays on the *cancha* to face the next team in rotation. The losing team goes to the back of the line.

I entered the Fronton Jai Alai to the din of the crowd, the reverberating metallic plop of balls hitting the walls, and the incessant cries of touts in red caps shouting out betting odds. Besides being a spectator sport, jai alai was, like about everything else in Havana, an excuse for gambling.

The stands facing the *cancha* were breathtakingly steep. Twenty rows high, each row of seats stood nearly two feet above the one below it, affording the spectators an almost unlimited view of the action. For safety's sake, they were separated from play by a net made of thin hemp twine. Cathedral windows ornamented each end of the fronton, and a glass roof heated the room like a greenhouse. Overhead, palm-frond ceiling fans rotated to keep the fusty air moving, however feebly.

The stands were filled with men wearing linen suits and straw hats, the women in cotton dresses. People mopped their faces with handkerchiefs. Scanning the crowd, I noted how many eyes glistened with adrenaline, as if anticipating a great disaster at any moment. They were seldom disappointed.

Behind the stands were open areas serving food, and a couple of bars. I walked into one of them. It was a good time to hit the bar, since it was usually deserted when players were on the *cancha.* I stepped up to the rail and ordered a Hatuey.

"I'm looking for someone," I said to the man when he returned with my drink. "Do you know Rico Gonzalez?"

"Of course, señor. Everyone knows Ricky!"

Ricky?

"Seen him lately?"

"Every day. You can see him, also. He's playing backcourt for the Blue Team, even as we speak. Will there be anything else, señor?"

I thanked him and walked back to the edge of the grandstands. A round of the match was underway, with one team in shimmering white trousers and white cotton shirts, and the other in the same trousers except they wore blue shirts. From the distance, I couldn't tell which of the blue-shirted players was Rico, but the bartender had said he was playing backcourt, so I took him at his word.

The action was furious, and the round was over in about fifteen seconds, after the white frontcourt player mistimed the return of the *pelota* and scooped it after a second brief bounce off the hardwood floor. One bounce was fine. Let the ball take two bounces, though, and you were . . . well, bounced.

White trotted off the *cancha,* while the two blue players grabbed up towels and wiped their faces as a team in green and yellow shirts took white's place. I glanced at the scoreboard, and noted that blue already had three points.

The blue backcourt player bent at the waist and worked to catch his breath. When he straightened, I recognized him as Rico Gonzalez.

Since I wouldn't have a chance to talk with him for a few minutes, I decided to take a seat in the stands and enjoy my beer.

The feeble efforts of the electric fans did little to stir the heavy, fetid air in the grandstands. A man at the top of the grandstand handed out paper fans on sticks, so I took one and grabbed a seat near the top row. Most people liked to sit down front, close to the action. I had always felt I could follow the game better from a distance. When something the size of a handball whizzes around a court at a hundred fifty miles per hour, there's something to be said for a wider perspective.

The beer was cold, which helped. On the *cancha,* the frontcourt player for the blue team served by running and swiping the *cesta* toward the far wall, launching the *pelota* into the air. It caromed off the end of the side wall, then against the far wall, before heading back toward the teams. The green-and-yellow backcourt player intercepted it at the right edge of the *cancha,* and the game was on.

Less than half a minute into the round, the backcourt player for the green-and-yellow team tried to cross from right to left, just as his frontcourt partner ran back for a high bounce. The frontcourt player swiped at the *pelota* at the same instant his teammate crossed the arc of his swing. The *cesta* smashed across the bridge of the backcourt player's nose, with a dull thud I could hear all the way to the back row of the grandstands, easily a hundred feet away. The backcourt player crumpled to the floor, as if the strings in his arms and legs had been cut. A small puddle of blood began to pool around his head. The officials quickly suspended play while the injured player was assisted off the *cancha* and the floor was cleaned. Since the green-and-yellow team had failed to make the play, blue took the point and advanced to the next round. The remaining green-and-yellow player walked back to the waiting pen, his face creased with anguish over what he had done to his partner.

Rico's blue team now had four points with only three needed to clinch the match. A red-shirted team took the court and positioned themselves to begin play.

Blue again served, and Rico's frontcourt partner placed the *pelota* squarely off the front wall, where it bounced back right between the four and seven lines. For almost half a minute the action was blinding, until the other team intercepted the ball and slammed it back to the front wall. Then, Rico Gonzalez saw an opportunity and attempted one of the most difficult shots in jai alai — the *chula.*

Red had bounced the ball off the lower part of the front wall, but with a backspin that arced it in a rainbow over the center of the *cancha.* Rico scooped it up on one bounce and then, as if swinging for the rafters, launched it high and tight down the middle of the court. It bounced off the top edge of the front wall and began a long, leisurely return trip down the entire length of the court, where it bounced off the back wall two inches from the floor. There was no way for the red team's backcourt player to field it in one bounce.

The crowd went nuts. They rose to their feet, stomped the grandstands, and chanted, "Ri-*cky,* Ri-*cky,* Ri-*cky*!"

I was impressed. In the six years I'd been away, Rico had turned into a star.

The game turned nasty on the next point. Blue remained on the *cancha* and an orange-shirted team took red's place. After several volleys back and forth, the orange backcourt player rocketed a shot low off the left wall. It bounced up, into the center wall, and then back toward the players. The orange frontcourt player inadvertently crossed in front of Rico, temporarily blocking his view, and the *pelota* took an ugly glance off the side of Rico's head.

The officials immediately called a foul, but that didn't help Rico. He had rolled into a fetal position on the *cancha,* cradling his head with both arms, as if he thought another shot was on the way.

It looked bad, but I'd been to enough matches that I knew it was just another day at the fronton.

I slipped a couple of five-peso notes to the attendant guarding the door to the locker rooms. Usually, no one could interact with the players, in order to prevent corruption. Like everything else in Havana, though, you could do pretty much anything you wanted by spreading around a little green.

Once in the locker room, nobody stopped me. Obviously, if I had gotten by the gatekeeper, I was okay.

I made my way to the back, where I found the blue-team doctor checking the goose-egg on the side of Rico's head. Rico had his back to me.

"I wouldn't worry," I said, as I watched. "Nothing to lose up there. Now, if it had hit him in the *cojones* —"

"I know that voice," Rico said.

He waved the doctor away and turned to me. In seconds, he was on his feet and he embraced me in a sweaty bear hug.

"Mac! It is true! At long last you have returned to Havana!"

He swayed on his feet like a punch-drunk fighter. The doctor and I caught him before he could collapse to the floor.

"You probably have a concussion," the doctor said. "And you are very lucky to walk away with only that. I have seen men die after being hit in the head with the *pelota.*"

Rico swiped at the air.

"It is nothing. A slug of fine Cuban rum, and I will be as good as new."

"Absolutely not," the doctor admonished him. "Not a drop of alcohol for you for at least two days."

At first, I thought Rico was going to argue, but then another wave of vertigo must have hit him, because I saw his eyelids flutter and his eyes started to roll.

"*Si.* When can I return to the *cancha*?"

"I won't allow you to play for at least a fortnight," the doctor told him. "Check in with me in a week and we'll see."

He turned to me. "You are this fool's friend?"

"I was at one time."

"We were like *brothers,*" Rico said, holding up two fingers pressed together. "Then he ran off to Miami and left me here in Havana to become a jai alai bum."

"So," the doctor said, again to me. "You are to blame. I'm surprised they allowed you back into the country. You have done the game of jai alai a huge disservice, señor!"

He smiled and held out his hand. "Keep this young idiot honest," he said, as we shook. "As I said, no alcohol for at least two days!"

He left me and Rico alone. Rico started to remove his shirt to take a shower.

"I heard you were here," he said.

"People like to talk."

"Those people say you are looking for a young girl."

"Who have you been talking to? I just got here yesterday."

"As it happens, I heard this from my sister-in-law. She told me she bumped into you last night at your hotel."

"It was an accident. I wasn't looking for her."

He waved at the air and gave me a conspiratorial smile.

"We will keep it between us. Tell me about this girl you are seeking."

I pulled one of Lila Hacker's pictures from my pocket.

"Seen her?"

He squinted at the picture for a moment.

"Hard to say. That *pelota* blurred my vision. Let me take a shower. We'll get something to eat and I'll take another look. How would that be?"

"It's exactly what I hoped," I told him.

Rico knew a place two blocks from the Fronton Jai Alai that he claimed served the finest *ropa vieja* in all of Havana. Since I had only sampled this island delicacy in places that admonished patrons not to spit on the floor, I took him at his word.

We left the fronton — I walked; Rico staggered — and crossed two streets over to a pink stucco building with a hand-hewn wooden sign and a couple of benches out front. The benches were full, and for a moment I thought I might have to support Rico's full weight to keep him from nosing over into the street while we waited for a table.

As soon as we crossed the front door, however, the maître d' rushed up to Rico and shook his hand.

"Welcome, Señor Gonzalez! Your table is waiting."

Rico winked at me, and the host led us to a table in the corner.

"This is your table?" I asked.

"It's an open table. Anytime I show up, they find a place for me, even if they have to move someone."

"You've gotten that famous in Havana?"

"My brother," he said. "Hector owns the restaurant."

The waiter brought us two glasses of water with lime wedges.

"We need rum! A toast to our reunion," Rico said, his voice slurred as if he had already killed half a bottle.

"You think that's smart? The doctor said you shouldn't —"

"Fucking doctors! What do they know? Does he have X-ray eyes? Can he see inside Rico's head? I think not. Fuck the doctor and fuck his sister!"

Several of the tables around us had gone silent. I leaned in toward him. "If you have a concussion, alcohol's a bad idea."

"Nonsense. I drink all the time."

He held up a hand, and the waiter appeared instantly by our table.

"A bottle of Bacardi," Rico said. "And two glasses. Some limes, a plate of them. We will eat *ropa vieja* and drink rum, eh?"

He reached across and slapped me on the thigh. The waiter wrote the order and disappeared into the kitchen by way of a passage behind the bar.

"This girl you're looking for," Rico said. "She has a name?"

"Lila Hacker, but she might be using a false identity here in Cuba."

"Show me her picture again."

I pulled a copy of Lila's picture from my pocket and held it out to him.

"Oh, my God! She is a looker. She is how old?"

"Fourteen."

"Fourteen! The fuck you say. I don't believe it. This girl is eighteen if she's a day."

"Her father says otherwise."

He stabbed at the picture with his index finger. "I don't give a damn if she is fourteen. You find this girl, I want to meet her. I'll give her something to take back to the States."

I glanced at the tables around us. Nobody wanted to look our way.

"So you haven't seen her?"

"Hell, no, Mac. But I'd like to. Here, let us drink to your successful search."

The waiter placed a bottle of Bacardi and a plate of lime wedges between us, and gave us each a glass.

"Your food will be out in a few moments," he said. "The chef is preparing it special for Señor Gonzalez and his esteemed guest."

"You hear that?" Rico said, after the waiter disappeared. "He fix it special for me and my esteemed guest. That is how they think of me here."

I suspected, if Rico acted this way every time he visited the joint, that fixing the *ropa vieja special* probably meant they were looking for the right cockroach to chop into the meat, but I didn't say this to him. Besides, in most Havana restaurants you were lucky *not* to get some insect parts with your meal.

Rico poured an inch of rum into my glass, and the same into his, and then squeezed the lime on top of it. I followed his lead. He held up his glass.

"To my American friend, Cormac Loame. We are reunited at long last."

"It isn't lucky to toast yourself," I warned him.

"Lucky! That's a good one. When was the last time you depended on luck? What everyone says is true, you know. Your luck is all bad . . . for other people."

He tossed back the rum, and for a moment his eyes glazed over. I sipped mine and waited for him to fall backward in his seat, as the alcohol finished off the job started by the *pelota.*

Soon, however, his eyes cleared, and he slapped the table. "Excellent! Here, Mac, finish your drink."

I shrugged and drank the rest of the rum. It was like fire running down my gullet, but I wasn't about to let Rico see that.

He poured another round, and we squeezed more lime into our glasses.

"When did you start playing jai alai instead of owning a team?" I asked, more to slow the drinking down than anything else.

"A couple of years ago. I was bored. My brother, that old burro, all he thinks about is work, work, work. I wanted to have a little fun, and then came the day when one of my players was injured on the *cancha.* I stepped in to take his place and the rest just happened."

The waiter brought our *ropa vieja,* shredded marinated flank steak with the ubiquitous black beans, yellow saffron rice, and fried plantains and cassava. The flank steak had been stewed in a spicy tomato sauce until it practically disintegrated.

Rico was right — it was the best I had eaten in Havana.

"What did I tell you?" he said.

"It's fine. You might want to throttle back

a little on the rum, though. You drink too much, I'll have to carry you home and I don't have a clue where you live these days."

"I live with Hector and Marisol. We have a big house over in Miramar, a few blocks from the water. You are right, though. I am beginning to feel a little dizzy. That *pelota* may have hit me harder than I thought. Where are you staying, Mac?"

"I'm at the Riviera."

"Ah, then you are only a few blocks from our home. You must come by for a visit."

"I don't think Hector would like that."

"What the fuck does he know? He's always at the Presidential Palace. I bet Marisol would love to see you. Eh? Eh? She's still —" He kissed the air.

"This is your sister-in-law we're talking about, Rico."

"Wha' the fuck? She is a woman, and I know a thing or two about women. She is married to Hector, but I do not believe they live as husband and wife. Do you know what I mean?"

"I'm not interested in family gossip."

He waved his hand in front of his chest. "Touchy. So long, and you still have feelings for my sister-in-law?"

"That's not the issue."

"So, come to the house. Marisol will be

there. Perhaps you can finish what you started so many years ago."

I wiped my mouth and placed my napkin on the table.

"Thanks for the meal, Rico. I admired your play today. You have the soul of a great jai alai player. I have work to do and not a lot of time to get it done. You have a nice evening."

I didn't wait for him to finish. Instead, I left the restaurant, and walked quickly down the street.

I wasn't sure why Rico set me off the way he did. I had only been in Cuba for a couple of days, but I had already become acutely aware that the Havana I had known in past visits was nothing more than a dimming memory. Marisol had become an upper-class concubine living, according to Rico, in a loveless marriage to a power-hungry sugar baron. Rico himself, once fun-loving and amiable, had become bitter and acerbic. It pained me to watch him fling himself into alcoholic dissolution.

The overwhelming sense of desperation about the place made it seem more edgy. The people, who by now certainly had realized that their entire way of life was in flux and about to change permanently and irretrievably, still clung tenaciously to their customs and diversions, with all the frenetic ardor of a jilted sweetheart.

The island was dying. In its final throes, it was shedding every part of it I had known. I didn't recognize the husk.

I spent the rest of the day, and most of the early evening, flashing Lila Hacker's picture around on the street, without a lot of success. It occurred to me that Lila had to have come through the same airport customs checkpoints that I had, and I had neglected to check there. I decided I would put that on my list for another day.

I ate an early dinner, played a few hands in the casino, and ended the day with a double bourbon neat in the bar. I saw Élan a couple of times, serving the other patrons. She winked at me once, but didn't make any attempt to talk with me directly, or start a conversation. That was fine with me. I was beat.

Chapter Eight

Jaime Guzman found me in the café off the hotel lobby the next morning. I had finished breakfast, and was enjoying a Cohiba with my coffee. As soon as I saw him coming my way, I knew I had stepped on somebody's toes.

Jaime sat across from me, and placed his hat on the table.

He gestured to the waitress, pointed to my coffee cup, and she scurried away to get one for him.

He pulled a card from his pocket and tossed it onto the table between us.

I didn't have to pick it up. I know my own business cards.

"You lost something, Mac?"

"I spread those around freely."

"I am going to mention a name, and I would like you to tell me what you know about him."

"Why?"

"You are in my country, *amigo.* Do not depend too strongly on our friendship. Until I say otherwise, you will answer the questions, not ask them."

I shrugged and took a sip of the coffee. The Cohiba beckoned, but I thought it might seem a little too aloof to blow smoke rings in the face of the local *policial.*

"Luis Gopaldo," he said.

"He's stringing for me. I need someone who knows the island, knows who's who. I used to use old Escobar."

Jaime shook his head. "Escobar. So sad. Is he dead yet?"

"I don't know. I haven't checked since a couple of days ago."

"Give me your gun, Mac."

"Like hell I will."

"Please," Jaime said, glancing left and right. I followed his gaze and saw he had the doors covered with plainclothes cops, the kind of guys who got hot and sweaty fantasizing about forcing answers with rubber hoses and brass knuckles in dark, cold rooms.

I shrugged and pulled my pistol from its holster under my left arm. I laid it on the table and slid it across to him.

He removed the magazine, cleared the round in the chamber, and fieldstripped the weapon on the placemat as quickly as any Marine gunny could have done. He picked up the barrel, and sniffed it.

"You have cleaned this weapon?" he asked.

"In Miami, before I left for Havana."

"You are certain?"

I nodded.

In less than a minute, he had the gun back together. I noted he didn't jack a round into the chamber.

"I will borrow this," he said.

"Customs is going to be upset if I don't have that when I leave the country."

"I will advise them if it comes to that."

"So, who did I shoot?"

He slipped the pistol into his jacket pocket. Out of the corner of my eye I saw the plainclothes guys relax. They looked disappointed.

"This morning police were advised of a body floating in the water down at the marina off the Calle del Prado."

"I know the place."

"It took five men to pull the body out of the water. His identification said he was Luis Gopaldo."

"And he had my card on him."

"Yes."

"I met with Gopaldo at El Floridita two days ago. Escobar's kid told me where to find him. I hired him to ask people questions."

"This missing fourteen-year-old girl?"

"Yes. I gave him some walking-around money and he left. I haven't seen him since. May I make an observation?"

"I would never dream of stopping you."

"My pistol is a thirty-eight. Whoever brought down Gopaldo would have had to use an elephant gun."

"So unkind," Jaime said.

"All right. It would have taken at least a forty-five — maybe even one of those new Magnums I've read about."

"We will try later today to retrieve the bullets that killed him. If they are thirty-eights, I will compare them to the rifling marks on your weapon. If they do not match, you can have this back."

"They won't. Don't fire it until you get the slugs out of Gopaldo, though."

"Why is this?"

"I don't want to waste any bullets. Once you see the lead it had to take to bring him down, you'll realize they couldn't have come from my gun. I only have a limited supply of ammunition in my suitcase upstairs and it's hard to come by in Havana right now."

Jaime thought it over. "In light of our

longstanding friendship," he said. "I will wait."

"One more thing. With Gopaldo dead, I'm fresh out of help with local knowledge. Do you know anyone I could trust to help me find out who's protecting McCarl, the man who has the girl?"

"I won't burn one of my own informants. I don't like you *that* much, *amigo.*"

"Couldn't hurt to ask."

"I will give you a couple of tips."

"I'll take what I can get."

"Your client works for Santo Trafficante."

"That's right."

"And, by extension, for Mr. Luciano."

"Also correct."

"Normally, the rival gangs keep things quiet between them in Havana. Live and let live, as you say."

"You're clearly thinking of someone else."

"As you *Americanos* say, then. They are rivals in money, but there is little open warfare. They constantly try to compete for the best acts in the lounges, the loveliest women in the casinos, but the real issue is money."

"It always comes down to that."

"Doesn't it? You and I, we have been in wars. We know what it smells like in the air on the day you are destined to lose. I smell it every day, lately. Mr. Trafficante and Mr. Lansky can smell it also. There has been a lot of money leaving Cuba in the last several weeks."

"How do you know this?"

"I have contacts down at customs — the same people who told me you were on the island."

"I was going to check with them today. I don't suppose by any chance that you've asked them about a couple of Americans who might have come through José Martí a week ago."

"What kind of police officer would I be if I had not asked about your young girl and her companion?"

"Nothing, huh?"

"It does not mean anything. So many people come. So many people go. The customs agents can be excused for not recalling all of them."

"I suppose you're right. At least you saved me a wasted taxi ride."

"I do hear stories about suitcases filled with *yanqui* dollars being loaded on private airplanes by the trailer load. I think the mobs are not ready to leave Havana, but they don't want to be loaded down if they have to make a quick exit. Do you understand?"

I remembered my impression from the first night I was in Havana.

"It's last call," I said.

"A colorful comparison."

"I don't see where that helps me."

"Simply this. Both Mr. Trafficante and Mr. Lansky are too busy right now to worry about some fourteen-year-old daughter of a minor gangland associate, even if he was once called *Madman.*"

"You're saying Trafficante and Lansky are dead ends."

"I would begin looking elsewhere."

"Where?"

"Has it occurred to you," Jaime said, "that McCarl might have brought the girl here specifically *because* of the unrest?"

"I don't follow."

"He knows Hacker can't follow him here, and because of his association with Hacker he also knows Trafficante isn't going to exert a great deal of effort to find him and the girl. It is possible that, at this moment in history, Cuba might be the safest place on earth for McCarl to bring an underage girl."

Chapter Nine

As soon as Jaime left, I returned to my hotel room and had the hotel operator place a cable call to Cecil Hacker. While I waited for the connection, I sat by the window, smoked a cigarette, and watched all the pretty boats plying the Caribbean beyond the stone walls ringing the Malecòn. I mused on how much more tranquil my life might be on one of them. Then the telephone rang and the operator told me Hacker was on the line.

"Have you found her?" he asked.

"No. I've been spreading pictures around. Someone doesn't want her found. A guy I hired to ask questions wound up dead in the water at the marina last night."

"You're getting close to her, then. He asked the right question to the wrong guy."

Hacker might have taken a lot of shots to the head in the ring, but it hadn't dimmed his thinking much. Some guys have thick skulls.

"Do you have that picture of McCarl? I could really use it."

"Yeah, we found one last night. He was part of my protection at a wedding last year, and he was in a couple of pictures. I sent a guy to Havana this morning to bring it to you."

"You could have wired a copy."

"It's not a great picture. I had a photography guy up here in Miami make a hundred copies. You should have them this afternoon."

"All right. Leave them at the front desk. I'll pick them up when I get back to the hotel."

"You have a lead?"

"I know where my stringer was found floating in the water last night. I'll start there."

The Riviera was situated at the corner of Calle del Paseo and the Malecòn. Gopaldo's body had been found at the marina at the end of the Calle del Prado, six or seven blocks over from Paseo. It was a nice day, so I decided to hoof it.

I didn't like poking around the marina unarmed, especially since it appeared Gopaldo had run into something nasty down there, but there was nothing for it. Until Jaime returned my pistol, I would have to resort to depending on my wits.

On the other hand, if I'd *had* any wits, I probably wouldn't have been in Cuba in the first place.

The marina wasn't much by Miami standards. It was mostly a lot of sailboats interspersed with the occasional working vessel. Some of the boats had been floating Cuba's waters since the Spanish-American War. I did see a few rumrunner speedboats left over from before the repeal of the Volstead Act. Now that their primary purpose had been obsoleted by long-delayed American reason, they sat slowly bobbing back and forth at their berths.

Whenever I found someone actually inhabiting a boat, I stopped to ask them about the murder the night before. For some, it was news. Others clearly knew about it, but had decided their lives would proceed more smoothly in a state of ignorance. A couple reported that they thought they had heard something, but couldn't be sure exactly when, or if they were actually gunshots and not just small fireworks.

I showed everyone I met Lila's picture. Nobody could recall having seen her.

I'd been walking the docks for almost an hour when I came across a thirty-eight-foot Wheeler Playmate moored to a rotting plank pier. The back half of the vessel was dominated by a wheelhouse and a covered galley. Forward of the wheelhouse, the owner had fitted a short flagpole to the top of the cabin. The top of the galley was open, with a ladder that jutted through the port to allow people access to the roof. Behind the outside wheel, and on either side of the ladder, was a pair of deck cots covered with rubber mattresses and tangled blankets. A deep-sea fishing chair was bolted to the hardwood deck, and in it sat the bearish man I'd met in El Floridita.

"Catch any?" I asked.

He belched and turned his head up to try to make me out from the sun at my back. He shaded his eyes with one hammy paw and squinted.

He wore the same clothes. From the stink that reached me even ten feet away, I had a feeling he'd slept in them overnight. Maybe over several nights.

"What's that?" he said.

"We met in El Floridita a couple of days ago. When you stumbled out, you said you had plans to go fishing. Wondered whether you'd caught any."

"Hell, man. I probably had all kinds of plans. El Floridita puts ideas in my head. I usually moor at Cojimar, but I was thirsty, so I sailed in to get a drink. That was . . . hell, some days ago."

"So you didn't take her out that night?" I said, gesturing toward the boat.

"In my condition? Might not be able to find my way home. You say we met in the bar?"

"You suggested I try a mojito."

"Couldn't have been me, then. Can't stand the damn things. Give me a daiquiri any day. You coming aboard or what?"

"I'm trying to find someone who might have heard gunshots around here last night."

He walked over to the gunwale and spat in the greasy water. "Gopaldo," he said. "You want to find out who killed him."

"So you know about it. Nobody else seems interested in talking about it."

"Superstitious provincial morons, the whole lot of them. I got some coffee brewed in the wheelhouse. You want some?"

"Don't mind if I do," I said, as I stepped down from the pier to the floating dock next to the transom. "Nice fishing boat."

"I've caught a few."

"What do you call her?"

"Pilar," he said, as he disappeared into the

wheelhouse. He returned several moments later with two mugs of coffee. He hadn't asked me whether I wanted cream or sugar. In his eyes, I don't suppose it mattered. If I had asked for them, I wouldn't have been his kind of man.

"Did you hear any shots?"

"No," he said. "Probably wouldn't have, all things considered. I imagine I was making some fair noise of my own, snoring on the bunk there."

He pointed toward the port cot.

"How did you find out about Gopaldo?"

He sipped at the coffee then said, "Saw them hoist him out of the drink. Awoke not long after dawn, felt the need to stretch my legs. Came up on the police and several laborers trying to drag Gopaldo out of the marina. Took nearly a platoon of them. Soon as I saw him I knew he was Gopaldo and he was dead. You ask me, somebody shot him somewhere else and dumped him in the water."

"How did you reach that conclusion?"

"You ask a lot of questions. What are you, some kind of cop?"

"Private cop. From Miami."

I handed him one of my cards. "Gopaldo was helping me find a girl from Miami. Since we're both speculating, I have a feeling he asked the wrong person the wrong question and it cost him his life."

"Damn shame. I liked Gopaldo. Man could drink. So he was working for you, eh?"

"Since about two days ago. I recruited him in the El Floridita. I used to work with a partner of his, man named Escobar."

"I know Escobar. Heard he was dead."

"Not yet, but he's giving it a game try. Don't suppose you know whether anyone might have borne Gopaldo any ill will."

"Half of Havana would have loved to kill the son of a bitch. Gopaldo and Escobar both became involved with one of the sugar barons and started collecting overdue debts. Escobar got sick and that made more work — and more money — for Gopaldo."

"Sugar barons?"

He nodded. "Worse than oil barons. Half the damn economy on this island is based on the rum trade. Can't make rum without sugar. There are four or five primary families who've divided up ninety-five percent of the production on the island. That much money can't help but lead to corruption. The sugar families have begun to intermingle with the criminal elements from the States. Sometimes it's hard to see where one business ends and the other begins."

I sipped some more coffee. It was strong

and a little bitter. I didn't mind. It helped me focus. As soon as he had mentioned the sugar producers, I'd started to feel a troubling buzz at the base of my neck. His last statement was almost exactly what Marisol Gonzalez had told me the previous evening regarding the intertwining of the mobs and Batista's government.

"You wouldn't know which of the plantation families Escobar and Gopaldo were working for, would you?" I asked.

"Sure. The Gonzalez family. They're top dogs in Havana right now."

I poured the rest of the coffee over the side. I had enough acid on my stomach already.

The Gonzalez family.

It figured.

"Don't suppose you have a gun I could borrow," I said as I handed the mug back to him.

Chapter Ten

He had guns.

He had a *lot* of guns.

"Come with me," he said, as he secured the hatch to the *Pilar*'s cabin. "We'll take my car. My house is ten minutes from here."

I followed him up the docks and to the street. It was close to noon, and the highway was filled with people rushing to lunch and a short siesta. We found his car. Moments later, we were in the swirl of the human parade.

"What on earth were you thinking, coming to Cuba without a gun?" he said, after we had left Havana.

"I had one. A thirty-eight automatic."

"What'd you do with it?"

"The police have it. They think I might have killed Gopaldo."

"With a thirty-eight?" he said, his voice reflecting incredulity.

"That was my argument."

"Shoot Gopaldo with a thirty-eight, he'd spit the bullets back at you."

"The police thought otherwise. I know the detective who's working the case. He'll get my gun back to me as soon as they know it wasn't the murder weapon."

He nodded, but without conviction. He knew the Havana police better than I did. I considered Jaime Guzman a grudging friend, but it had been a few years since I'd crossed the Florida Straits. Things change.

We entered the small village of San Francisco de Paula. The man pointed to a Spanish colonial house a block up the street.

"My place. We can find you a sidearm there."

The place looked familiar. In one respect, it was no different than any of a hundred other colonials on the island. On the other hand, I was sure I'd seen it before.

Then it hit me.

"Wait a minute," I said, as I reached out and grabbed his arm. I took a hard look at his face. "Jesus, I'm an idiot," I said. "You're Hemingway."

"You didn't know that?"

"Not until this moment. You aren't . . . that is . . ."

"Not what you expected?"

"No."

He patted my hand on his arm. "I get that a lot."

He parked on the street, and I followed him up the short drive to his home. A small sign outside the door read *Finca Vigia.* After years in South Florida and a number of trips to Cuba, I had enough Spanish to know that it translated, roughly, to Lookout Farm.

The exterior, once we were up close, was a little shabby. Nothing, however, prepared me for what was inside.

As soon as he opened the door, a wave of ammonia swept through the jamb. Two cats bolted into the yard.

"You like cats?" he asked, as he held the door open for me.

I walked into the house. The walls were plaster, with arched portals leading from room to room. The floor was an expensive Mexican tile. It seemed every second wall was there for the sole purpose of supporting bookcases crammed with all sorts of volumes. The other walls were decorated with hunting trophies — a mounted Thompson's gazelle, a bighorn elk, two or three pronghorn antelopes. Everywhere I looked I saw a cat — often two or three — lounging.

The furniture was mostly rough-hewn, with several more comfortable overstuffed chairs scattered about. I saw paintings by artists whose names I vaguely recognized, and I thought they looked strangely out of place amongst the shabby, masculine surroundings.

"Mary!" Hemingway shouted as he closed the door, almost crushing one of his pets. "I think we need some drinks. What do you think, Loame? Mary! Where in hell are you, woman?"

A man's voice from the back of the house said, "Shut up, you old goat! People are trying to sleep around here." He had a faint Irish accent.

Hemingway put a finger to his lips. "The lodger in the guest house. Hangover. Poor devil lives with a perpetual one, these days. For that matter, so do I. You want a beer?"

It seemed impolite to turn down a Nobel laureate.

He disappeared for a moment, and then returned with two bottles of Hatuey.

"Have a seat," he said, pointing to one of the chairs. "It isn't every day I get to talk with a private eye. People think I hate them, because of that thing with Spillane."

"Spillane who?"

He stared at me and then roared. His head tilted back and he laughed like a hyena. "Spillane who! Damn, that's smart. You have a quick mind. I like that."

I didn't have a clue what he found so funny.

"So, Loame," Hemingway said, "who do you plan to shoot with my gun?"

I took a sip of the Hatuey. "I don't plan to shoot anyone. I've shot enough people in my life, especially here in Cuba. If I shoot any more, they may never let me come back."

"Doesn't make a damn bit of difference. Another couple of weeks and there won't be a country to come back to. Guevara and Castro and their red pals will reach Havana by the end of the month. When your detective friend gives you back your gun, talk him into going back to Miami with you. The revolution comes and there are going to be a lot of badges up against the walls."

"I don't see you packing to escape," I said, waving a hand around the room.

"I'm *Papa!* Haven't you heard? I get a pass. Hell, I've nearly lost count of the insurrections I've survived. *By my troth, I care not; a man can die but once; we owe God a death . . . and let it go which way it will, he that dies this year is quit for the next.*"

"Shakespeare?"

"Hemingway, damn it!" he said, pounding the table with one meaty paw. Then he seemed to mellow. "Well, Hemingway by way of Shakespeare, now that I think of it. Stole the damn line. Used it in one of my books. Now which one was it? Never mind. This damned country owes me, Loame. That boat you found me on today? I used it during the war to hunt out Nazi submarines. Let the damned reds come. Nobody hates Nazis like the reds hate Nazis. They won't bother me. Now, do you want that gun or don't you?"

He didn't wait for an answer. Instead, he drained his beer, stood and left the room. I heard him opening and closing doors in the next room, which I thought was a library. When he returned, he carried several parcels wrapped in oily muslin cloth.

"Here's a fine piece," he said, unwrapping the first bundle. He held up a nasty-looking weapon. "Luger Parabellum, in seven-point-six-five. This gun is as clean as the day I liberated it. It was in France, a place called Villedieu-les-Poêles, not long after D-Day. Were you in the war, Loame?"

"Yes."

"Ah, then you know. In Villedieu-les-Poêles I heaved a couple of grenades down into a cellar infested with SS officers. This gun belonged to one of them. Couldn't tell you to this day which one. Have some rounds for it lying around here somewhere —"

"I don't think it will fit in my holster." I pulled my jacket back to show him. I didn't mention that I wasn't fond of the idea of traipsing around Havana with a Luger strapped to my side.

"Daresay it won't. Well, then, perhaps you can make use of this one."

He unwrapped a Colt 1911 automatic. There were patches of what I hoped was only rust on the handle. He pulled back the slide. There was a grating sound.

"Now, that's embarrassing," he said. "Disgraceful. I usually take better care of my arms, but since . . . since . . . well, for a few years now I seem to forget things. That ever happen to you?"

"Sure," I said.

"How do you feel about revolvers?"

"I've fired a couple in my day."

"Smith and Wesson thirty-eight Special," he said, unwrapping the third bundle. "Now, this is a private dick's gun. You like the thirty-eights, don't you? Wasn't that what you used to plug old Gopaldo?"

"I didn't shoot Gopaldo. You're confused."

"No doubt," he said, as he leaned forward and cradled his forehead in one of his palms. "Of course you didn't shoot Gopaldo. He was working for you. What sense would that make? But you do shoot a thirty-eight, right?"

"I do."

"Good enough. See if this will fit that fancy shoulder rig of yours."

He handed the bundle over to me. I pulled the muslin from the weapon and placed it on the table.

The gun was a World War II–era Victory Model, a lend-lease piece in the four-inch barrel, similar to the Model 10 used by most policemen in the States. It still had the lanyard loop screwed into the butt. The handle was mahogany, oxidized nearly black by years of weather, and smoothed by handling.

There were rounds in the cylinder. I removed them, lined them up on the muslin, and then I checked the action. The cylinder spun freely on a well-oiled spindle. The hammer action made a satisfyingly solid click when I pulled it back.

I was careful not to dry-fire it. I had a feeling Hemingway wouldn't appreciate me mistreating a firearm. I eased the hammer back down, loaded five of the .38 Special cartridges back into the cylinder, and closed the gun with the hammer on the empty chamber.

It slid into my shoulder holster like a bum into the first bed he'd seen in months. It felt like it belonged there.

"Nice piece," I said. "You want to sell it?"

"We'll call it a loan," Hemingway said. "Want to tell me why you need it?"

"It's a long story," I said, as I took a pull from the Hatuey.

"Do I look like I'm in a hurry?"

I shrugged. I owed it to him. He had given me the gun, after all.

"As soon as you mentioned the sugar barons, something clicked in my head. It occurred to me that Gopaldo might not have been killed because he asked the wrong people about Lila Hacker and Danny McCarl. It's possible he was murdered because he was working for me."

"I don't understand."

"You said Gopaldo and Escobar worked for the Gonzalez family. I have a history with one of them, young Hector."

"I know Hector Gonzalez."

"From what I hear, a lot of people know him. Back in fifty-two, I was in Havana doing a skip trace for a bail bondsman in Miami. Normally, I wouldn't leave the country for a case like that, but there was a lot of money involved. The bond was over twenty thousand dollars. The skip had been running a bookie joint out of a hotel room in the Breakers. He got popped, and after he made bail he took a boat to Cuba and disappeared. The ten percent finder's fee to bring him back was a hell of an incentive to hop over to the island, so I took the job."

"This bail bondsman thought you could drag a man from Cuba back to Miami against his will?"

"What can I say? When you want thuggery done, you go to the head thug. It was my third trip to Havana. The second time I'd been here, I'd met a girl. Her name was Marisol. We went well together, if you know what I mean. I had to leave the island in a hurry that time, and it was a while before it was safe for me to come back."

"It sounds as if there's a story in that by itself."

"There is, but it doesn't have anything to do with the Gonzalez family. When I came back, in fifty-two, I spent most of my time looking for my skip, and in my spare moments I asked around about Marisol. I finally found her. It had been four years since we had been together. She was working as an accountant for one of the clubs. She was also seeing Hector Gonzalez."

"A love triangle."

"Something like that. I think she never

expected to see me again, after the way I had to run back to the States. She wasn't interested in becoming an American, so there was this divide between us. The minute I laid eyes on her, six years ago, it was like the years fell away. Hector ran across us in a nightclub over off the Prado. He had been drinking and he thought I was trying to steal his girl."

"Which you were."

"Well, yeah, but I didn't expect him to take it so personally. Hector decided to make a beef of it and we got into a fight. I'm a much better fighter than Hector. He didn't do so well. Marisol and I took off for a villa in Bahia, spent three or four days there making up for the years apart. I won't go into details. I had left word with Escobar on how to reach me. He'd been bird-dogging my skip and finally ran him down at a pension in La Palma. The only problem — and I didn't know this at the time — was that he had been put there by some local mob guys associated with his boss in Miami."

"You walked into a trap."

"Not a trap, exactly. That kind of stuff happens mostly in the movies. I didn't expect him to have the kind of protection around him that he did, though. I told Marisol I'd be back, and I took a car to La Palma. Getting in to my skip was the easy part. Getting him out proved a little tougher. There was a fight. Gunplay. I got hit in the calf, took another in the ass."

"You got shot in the ass?" Hemingway laughed.

"It wasn't funny at the time. Hurt like hell. Thankfully, it was a small twenty-five slug, and it had already ricocheted off the wall behind me before it hit me. So I took a little incidental damage. The guys shooting at me . . . well, their damage was anything but incidental. I knew I was hot, and if I showed up in Havana I'd either be arrested or rubbed out, so I took my skip to the local airfield, hired a single-engine plane and a pilot, and had him fly me across the Florida Straits to Key West."

"Thrilling."

"You sort of had to be there. I turned my skip over to the local jail in Key West, got myself patched up, and then contacted Jaime Guzman with the Havana police to explain things. The guys I'd shot were *yanqui* thugs, the kind of people nobody would miss. Cuba was glad to have them out of its hair, but Jaime suggested that I might want to stay stateside for a while. I haven't been back here since."

"You left the girl."

"I left her without even saying good-bye. I tried to get a message to her, but I think Hector might have intercepted it. After I wrote her two or three times and never got an answer, I figured it was time to move on."

"You just gave up on her?"

"There wasn't much I could do. She was in another country, one I didn't dare enter until the heat was off. Either she got my messages and had decided I was a hopeless case, or someone kept them from her and there wasn't anything I could do about that. There wasn't much I could do at all."

"And now?"

"Someone has taken note that I'm back in the country. I found a radio transmitter taped to the back of my headboard in my hotel room yesterday. I ran into Marisol at the casino in the Riviera a couple of nights ago. Jaime Guzman had already told me she had married Hector Gonzalez after I bolted six years ago, so I was a little surprised to see her in the hotel, dolled up like an MGM movie star.

"At first, I thought it was an accident, meeting like that. After a while I began to think otherwise. Marisol told me Hector is all tied up with Batista, and I've also heard that the sugar barons are mixed in with the mobs. The mobs, Batista, the sugar families, it all makes for a dangerous triangle. Also, if meeting Marisol wasn't an accident, it means Hector knows I'm in the country."

"And you think he found out from Gopaldo."

"Given that, shortly afterward, Gopaldo was sucking bilge water in the marina. That was my thought, yes."

Hemingway slouched in his chair and took a drag from his beer. "Hector Gonzalez doesn't like you."

"Hector Gonzalez would like to toss me under a train," I corrected. "I showed him what a first-class beating feels like. He's had six years to think about how he'd like to return the favor. This is no time for me to walk into dark places in Havana without a gun."

"He'd kill Gopaldo for working for you?"

"He might. Six years ago, Hector was mean-tempered. Now he has a little power. That could make him dangerous. Gopaldo may have thought he was doing Hector a favor, telling him about meeting up with the tough *yanqui* in El Floridita. He probably had no idea how much Hector hates me."

Hemingway drained the rest of the beer,

set the bottle on the table, and crossed his hands over his rotund belly.

"Some story," he said. "Are you open to advice?"

"I'm open to *good* advice."

"Go home. Get the hell out of Dodge. This place is too hot for you. Go back to Miami and tell your client to send some other thug down here to find his daughter."

"I can't do that."

"Hell, Loame, this whole island is about to go up in flames! Even as we sit here slamming back Hatueys, Castro and his boys could be storming the Presidential Palace. In a week or two, every American in Cuba will be tossed out. For all you know, McCarl and this girl have moved on already."

"I don't think so. I think they came to Cuba because McCarl knew he would be protected here. Somebody has him hidden, or has put a shield up around him. He wouldn't leave Cuba unless he was forced out."

"But you don't know who might be protecting him."

"Not yet. I will, though. Sooner or later."

"Better make it sooner," he said. "Come on. I'll drive you back to the city."

Chapter Eleven

Hemingway dropped me off at the Riviera before heading toward his boat at the marina. He offered some cautionary last words.

"Find that girl and get off the island, if you insist on staying. I'm not kidding, Loame. An insurrection is an ugly thing. You don't want to be around when the reds march into town."

He didn't wait for an answer.

The lobby of the Riviera was cool and smelled of ozone when I walked through the front doors.

I was intercepted almost immediately.

I had stopped at the front desk to see if the package of photos from Miami had been delivered, and two guys stepped up from behind and stood on either side of me. They were classic goon types — strong of back and weak of mind, which usually meant they didn't think much before kicking the shit out of you.

"Alguien desea verme?" I asked, in Spanish.

"Cut that babaloo shit," one of them said — clearly the articulate one. "You have an appointment."

"Must have forgotten."

The desk clerk had disappeared. I didn't think he was looking for my package.

"Let's go," I said.

They led me to the elevator. Once the doors had closed, one of them held my arms back while the other took Hemingway's revolver from my holster. I'd had my hardware lifted twice in one day. I didn't like it much, but I decided to ride this out and see where it led.

Who knew? Maybe I'd learn something useful.

That would be a nice change.

One of the thugs put a key in the control pad of the elevator and turned it to *Express.* That meant we were headed for the top floor. I was beginning to miss elevator operators.

The doors opened and they marched me into a short hallway that led to a large, open room with windows on three sides. The furniture was modern and comfortable. Sheer draperies hung in sliding doorways billowed as the ocean breezes from the Malecòn transected the room.

"Wait here," the loquacious one said.

"No problem."

There were a couple of magazines on the table in front of me. I picked one up and glanced through it, even as I cased the room.

There were damned few avenues of escape. The Riviera was a high-rise hotel. I could always get out through one of the sliding doors, but I wasn't sure that was a preferable alternative to sitting still and taking a bullet.

The only way out was the elevator. With the quiet guy blocking the door, that meant there wasn't any way out.

Okay. I was strapped in for the whole ride.

I flipped through the magazine, pretending to read, until the talkative mug came back into the room.

"Come with me," he said.

I didn't say anything. I rose and followed him down the hallway to another room that looked exactly like the one I had just left. It occurred to me that this penthouse had been carved out of two separate suites.

Two men sat on a couch in the next room. A third man sat on a chair perpendicular to the couch. The third man looked like a midget accountant. He smoked a cigarette. The two men on the couch looked me over as I walked into the room.

Hemingway's revolver lay on the coffee table.

I wasn't invited to sit.

"Mr. . . . Loame, is it?" asked one of the men on the couch — the one on the left.

"Cormac Loame," I said.

"How do you like your room?"

"It's peachy. Who do I thank for the upgrade?"

"That would be me. I'm Harry Smith. I manage the hotel."

"Thanks, then. I'm sorry to disappoint you, Mr. Smith, but I'm afraid I'm not much of a gambler. You might have lost money comping me to a nicer room."

"Oh, I think you like to take your chances. You came into my hotel with a gun."

"That?" I said, pointing to the revolver on the table. "It's a loaner. The police have *my* gun."

"Could you tell us exactly why you are in Havana?"

"I'm on business. I've been sent to Havana to take someone back to Miami."

"With a gun?"

"The gun isn't for the person I'm taking back. It's for the person who might try to stop me from taking her back."

Smith pulled a cigarette from a tulipwood

box sitting on the coffee table, and lit it. He took the time to blow one voluminous cloud of smoke into the air.

"I'm intrigued. Tell me more."

I told him about Cecil Hacker, his daughter Lila, and about Danny McCarl.

"Cecil Hacker works for Santo Trafficante," Smith said.

"That didn't come up when he hired me, but I've heard it."

"You could have stayed at the Sans Souci. Trafficante owns that hotel. You might have saved yourself a lot of money."

"It's not my money. I've stayed at the Sans Souci. It's a nice place. Havana isn't Vegas, though. The gambling isn't regulated here. I heard Mr. Lansky runs a fair table at the Riviera."

The small man sitting to the side coughed briefly. I think he was swallowing a chuckle.

"I'm sorry, Mr. Lansky," I said. "I meant no offense."

Lansky's eyes narrowed a bit. Maybe he had hoped I wouldn't recognize him. Hell, I guess you run across dozens of five-foot Jewish guys every day on the top floor of the Riviera.

Smith tapped an ash from his cigarette into the cut-glass ashtray next to the revolver. "I'm not certain what to do with you,

Mr. Loame. I suppose I could have Johnny and Jules chuck you out the window onto the Malecòn, but rush-hour traffic is already bad enough in Havana."

He waited for a second, as if expecting a laugh or two from the other guys in the room. When it didn't come, his face grew dark. "Here's how things are going to happen," he said. "Fair or not, the tables at the Riviera aren't interested in your money. I've taken the liberty of booking a room for you at the Sans Souci. It's a nice room. I suggest you use it for as few nights as possible, then return to Miami."

"After I find Lila Hacker."

"Find your girl and go home, Mr. Loame. Havana is a dangerous place, especially right now. I don't have the time to worry about some two-bit private cop running around my hotel with a gun, or the bad publicity you could bring to this establishment if you happened to shoot someone on the premises. Do I make myself clear?"

"You want me to blow."

"Then we have an understanding." He gestured to Johnny and Jules. "These gentlemen will escort you to your room, watch you pack your bags, and then will go with you to the lobby. To show you there are no hard feelings, I've arranged for a car to take you to the Sans Souci."

"The gun?" I said, pointing at it with my chin.

"They will return it to you when they deliver you to the hotel."

I straightened my jacket and reminded myself to breathe.

"One question," I said.

"I have no desire to become part of your investigation," Smith said.

"Hold on," Lansky said. "I'm interested. Let him ask."

Smith looked a little irritated, but he also knew who paid the bills. Lansky had been used to getting what he wanted since Prohibition, and Smith wasn't about to stand in his way.

"All right, then, Mr. Loame. Your question?"

"With all due respect, I came to Havana under the impression that McCarl may have brought Lila Hacker here because he knew that — wherever he was going — Mr. Trafficante's men couldn't touch him. That would mean someone is protecting him. What I'm wondering is, who in Havana could do that?"

"I'll answer that," Lansky said. "Nobody. This is about family, Loame. There are rules. Even though the Madman isn't high in the Trafficante organization, he's an associate, and family members of associates are off limits. If one of Mr. Hacker's employees made off with his daughter against her wishes, then he would have no protection at all in Havana from anyone in our business."

"What about from the Cubans themselves?"

He shrugged his tiny shoulders. "The Cubans' business is the Cubans' business."

"Meaning they could only protect him as long as Mr. Trafficante didn't know they were protecting him."

"Meaning," Lansky said, "that *the Cubans' business is the Cubans' business.* I'm sure you can appreciate, under the circumstances, that we are very busy. Please enjoy your stay at the Sans Souci, Mr. Loame, and good luck in your search."

One of the thugs — Johnny or Jules — grabbed my arm. It felt like someone had rolled a Cadillac over it. The other guy picked up the gun and stuffed it in his pants, under his jacket.

None of the big guys in the suite said good-bye.

Chapter Twelve

Somehow, I had crossed a line.

This was one of the reasons I hated going to Cuba and avoided it every chance I got — unless, of course, there was a new Buick Roadmaster in the balance.

Havana was nothing but a huge closed club for the bent-nose crowd, the plantation playboys, and every celebrity on the downhill side of the arc of fame in the Western Hemisphere. Guys like Trafficante and Lansky and Sam Giancana, and even local boys like Hector Gonzalez, had taken paradise and had turned it into a bordello.

People who revel in filth don't like to let in the light. When an outsider, like me, starts poking his nose under the harem tent, it draws attention. At chichi social clubs in the States, that can lead to a rough ejection by the well-groomed bouncers who double as masseurs and bartenders and maître d's.

In Havana you're as likely to learn you've

irritated the wrong guy about the same time the cinderblocks and chains strapped to your feet hit the coral bed of the Caribbean a couple of miles off the Malecòn.

I won't deny it. When Johnny and Jules unceremoniously shoved me out of the elevator into the Riviera penthouse, I knew I was in for the treatment. I was certain more than one SOB had taken the express flight to the parking lot, off the balcony.

What I hadn't expected was what waited for me when the boys dropped me off at the Sans Souci. They pulled up in front of the hotel, and immediately a bell captain jumped to open the door.

"Señor Loame," he said. "What a pleasure to have you with us at the Sans Souci. My name is Elio Cruz."

I took his hand. I'm sure my eyes told him exactly how puzzled I was. His own eyes widened as one of Lansky's messenger boys handed Hemingway's revolver to me, and I slid it into my shoulder holster.

People see a lot of stuff in Cuba. Cruz recovered quickly, his grin returning to his brown little face. "If there is anything you need," he said, "please feel free to call the front desk and ask for me personally. Mr. Trafficante has directed me to provide you with any comforts required. May I show you to your room?"

As he spoke, Lansky's muscle slid back into their Caddy and peeled out of the turnaround back out onto the highway.

Putting me at the Sans Souci had been a stroke of genius. Not only did it remove me from under Lansky's nose, it also removed me from about everything useful. The hotel had been constructed some distance from downtown Havana, perhaps because Trafficante hadn't wanted prying eyes. The taxi fares alone were going to break me. I hadn't been lying about Lansky's fair tables, but it was one of the other reasons I had chosen to stay at the Riviera.

"Yeah, Elio," I said. "There is something you can get me."

"And what is that, señor?" he asked, almost begging.

"Call and make me reservations at the Hilton."

I think I hurt Elio's feelings. I don't think it mattered much. I had a hard time imagining collusion between Trafficante and Lansky, even with rumors floating around that Trafficante had some financial interest in the Riviera.

Trafficante's feigned attempt to flatter and coddle me was transparent. First, he wanted to please Cecil Hacker, whose tax problems almost certainly involved some of Santo's money. Also, there was the strong possibility that he wanted to keep me on a short leash.

I couldn't do my job if my center of operations was only slightly less in the boonies than a sugar plantation. The action on this case was obviously in Havana. So was the Hilton, only a few blocks from Lansky's other Havana enterprise, the Hotel Nacional. I'd have preferred to stay at the Nacional, but I'd already been kicked out of one Lansky joint. The decision was obvious.

I didn't think I had to worry about hacking off Trafficante. If everything I'd heard since my arrival about the advancing threat of the Twenty-Sixth of July Movement was true, he had a lot more on his plate than one irritating private investigator. I was betting I'd never be missed.

Elio made the call and hailed a taxi for me. I asked him to send my bags over to the Hilton. Then I slipped him a twenty for his trouble. It was more than he probably made in the typical week. He was only too happy to accommodate me.

The taxi fought traffic all the way into the Vedado district of central Havana. The driver had a radio on, tuned to Radio Rebelde, though he kept the volume down so people outside the cab wouldn't know he was listening to a clandestine station.

I could follow enough of the broadcast to catch that Guevara had captured the town of Fomente and that someone named Wieland from the State Department in Washington had given Batista the official kiss-off from the White House. Obviously, Eisenhower had decided that simply cutting off arm sales to Cuba hadn't sent a strong enough message. He had finally decided to set Fulgencio adrift entirely.

I knew what that meant, of course. Without the threat of retaliation from the US, the rebels would overrun Havana in a matter of days rather than weeks. Batista was probably already packing the good silver and scoping out waterfront property in Bolivia. I'd read a lot about him and the way he had run the country, and I didn't take him for the type who was eager to make a last stand. I didn't like the idea of being caught flat-footed in Havana when the reds marched up the Prado. I had to step up my hunt for Lila Hacker.

The cabbie dropped me at the front door of the Hilton. I was impressed by the modern architecture and the opulence of the place. It was Conrad Hilton's great misfortune to have sunk a small fortune into building his new Caribbean pleasure palace only nine months before the revolution shifted up into the full-tilt boogie-woogie. Everything gleamed, from the glittering glass to the chrome trim on the doors and windows.

The air in Havana was about two thirds water and a quarter dust, so it was a welcome relief when I walked through the doors into the chilled, marble-floored lobby. The boy at the front desk had the reservation Elio Cruz had phoned in from the Sans Souci. I asked for a tenth-floor room overlooking the Malecòn, because I had grown accustomed to the finer things in life and I was spending Hacker's money. I figured he owed to me for the inconvenience of having to cross the Florida Straits.

I pocketed my key and wandered into the bar. It was past noon, which made it post time in my book, and I wanted to cut the dust of the day from my throat with another Hatuey. As soon as I took the first sip, I realized I was hungry, so I crossed the lobby to the restaurant and took a table directly underneath an ungodly-sized ceiling fan. I thought the restaurant's tiki culture design was nauseating, but I figured I could put up with it long enough to choke down some ham and eggs.

As I waited for my food, I reviewed what I knew.

It wasn't a hell of a lot.

At first, I had been convinced Gopaldo had been murdered because he asked the wrong guy — or guys — about Lila Hacker. Now that I knew he was also working for Hector Gonzalez, who would gladly feed me face-first into an airplane propeller, I had to acknowledge the possibility that Gopaldo had simply chosen the wrong side and told the wrong person about it.

I had also hoped Danny McCarl had brought Lila to Havana with the expectation of protection, presumably from Meyer Lansky who, despite some tangential mutual business dealings with the Luciano family, had no real affection for Santo Trafficante. Lansky himself had told me he wasn't protecting McCarl. While I had learned some time in the past not to put too much faith in the word of gangsters, my instincts told me Lansky told the truth. He had bigger fish to fry.

At the same time, he had been afraid of the bad press I might bring down on him if I opened fire on someone in the lobby of the Riviera. That told me either he had some idea of who might be protecting McCarl, or that my reputation in Cuba was a lot tougher than I had imagined.

Lansky as much as told me that Trafficante wasn't involved, and that made sense, considering that Hacker worked for Santo. I couldn't think of any reason why Trafficante would aggravate Hacker by protecting his daughter's abductor, especially when the Feds were so eager to make Hacker talk about his dealings with Luciano family money.

Then there was Hemingway's theory that the real power in Cuba derived from the sugarcane, and I should be looking toward the sugar barons instead of American wiseguys.

What the hell. I had struck out so far working my side of the Florida Straits. It was time to start trolling the natives.

I inhaled my lunch. Then I made my way to my room. They had given me something called a "junior suite," which meant there was a couch in the room along with the bed and there was a long, eight-foot-deep balcony overlooking the water.

When I opened the door, I found my bags sitting next to the bed. Elio Cruz had earned his tip. Whoever had dumped my luggage had also cranked up the air-conditioning. I was suddenly overcome with fatigue. I figured a drowsy detective is a lousy detective, so I flipped off my shoes, stripped down to my skivvies, and lay on the bed for a quick half-hour catnap.

There's this dream that comes to me from time to time, and it paid me a visit while I snoozed in my junior suite on the tenth floor of the Havana Hilton.

I'm a young boy, ten or eleven. It's winter, someplace really cold, which is strange because I never lived anyplace north of Charleston, South Carolina, when I was a kid. I'm there nonetheless, bundled to within an inch of my life to ward off the frigid temperatures. I'm wearing one of those leather caps with the flaps that roll down to cover your ears, and a pair of gloves that look like something Nanook of the North might have made from seal skins.

I never know how I got there, but I'm standing out in the middle of a frozen lake, a hundred yards from any solid land, and I'm all alone. I turn all the way around, until I get back to the place where I started, and there's not a soul in sight. It's snowing, and the wind whips across the ice, and when it blows across my ears all I can hear is the *whoosh* of zero-degree air.

The lake is ringed by evergreens, but they're coated in a glassy shell by the freezing rain and sleet and snow, and some of them have even been bent over almost all the way to the ground under the weight of the accumulated ice.

I stand there for a moment, wondering if I'm the last living being on earth. Then I hear a *snap.* At first I think it's one of the trees on the shore. I look down, and I see a jagged scar arc across the frozen lake from a point in front of my toes.

I hear another whipcracking sound, and when I turn I can see an identical fracture run out from behind me.

I know what is happening, but I'm powerless to stop it and too scared to run.

Within seconds there's a staccato chorus of snaps and creaks and splitting sounds, and I realize that the ice beneath me is disintegrating in thousands of hairline fissures. I look down and find the *Boy Scout Handbook* has miraculously appeared in my hands. I try to look up what to do when a frozen lake begins to disintegrate beneath your feet, but every time I try to read the page with the information that will save my life, the words and letters drip from it like rainwater off a roof.

Now I'm shivering, more from terror than the cold, and there is a final, extended shriek from the ice, and I'm falling for what seems like forever, the numbing water below the ice swallowing me, first the knees, then my waist, and finally I'm below the ice. The frigid water hits my face, and I reflexively gasp, and choking icy blackness fills my mouth and lungs, and it's only seconds before my legs won't do anything I tell them to do.

I flail my arms, trying to propel myself back up to the surface. When I finally reach it, it's as if the lake has healed itself in mere seconds, and my head bumps against a solid, inch-thick barrier of ice that stands between me and survival. My arms grow thick and slow, but I still struggle, beating my tiny childish fists against the sheet, trying to break through to the life-giving air that I can see mere inches from my face.

It's useless, though. The ice is too thick and too heavy, and I'm too small and weak to defeat it, and it slowly dawns on me that I'm not going to win this one. This is when the drowning begins, when I give up and resign myself to the inevitable.

Then I see a shadow cross the ice. It comes to rest right above me. With one more desperate effort, I throw myself toward the ice, and beat against it with my hands and feet. There's someone right above me. My only hope is that he can hear or see me and can find a way to break a hole in the ice for me to escape.

I can tell the person knows I'm down here. He bends over as I flatten my face against the ice and flail at it with my nearly useless hands.

At the last second, as the edges of my vision begin to crinkle and flash, I recognize the person peering at me through the tunnel of light left to my oxygen-starved brain.

I stare through the ice at my own face.

Somehow, even as my life is fading away in the arctic water beneath the ice, I stand on the frozen lake above and watch myself drown.

And, in the instant before I wake, I hear an ominous *crack . . .*

I'm an educated guy. I know about Freudian imagery and defense mechanisms and latent dream interpretation. I'm not an expert in that field, since I'm not a psychiatrist and never hoped to be one, but I've read a few books, so it isn't hard for me to figure out where this dream comes from.

Even so, it doesn't stop me from lurching forward each time the ice cracks under the weight of me watching myself drown, in a final effort to survive, and that's exactly what I did.

■ ■ ■ ■

Okay, so sleep wasn't such a great idea.

I pulled on my pants, slipped my shirt on but left it unbuttoned, and lighted a cigarette before stepping out onto my balcony. The waters beyond the Malecòn were a transparent, unnatural shade of greenish blue, almost like the transparent luster of a perfect aquamarine gem. All sorts of boats bobbed in the waters and for a moment I wished again to be on any one of them, rather than where I was, trying to shift rocks around in my thick head.

I only have the dream when I am overwhelmed, when I am no closer to solving a case than when I had started, and the clock is ticking. It's like some kind of referee in my head, telling me that I need to step it up or forfeit the game.

It was time to start earning Cecil Hacker's money.

Chapter Thirteen

I took a long shower, turning the water as far to the scalding side of the faucet as I dared, and then took a bracing cold rinse. The effect got my heart beating again, forced oxygen to my lazy brain, and gave me a fresh start on the lengthening day.

My leg man in Havana was dead. I couldn't do anything about that. Hemingway was convinced that my real problems lay with the plantation owners, who surely faced significant problems of their own should Fidel and his jungle guerillas scorch their path all the way to the sea.

Maybe, I reasoned, I had a chance to make some inroads with the locals while their attention was diverted to the south.

I checked in at the front desk, but the clerk there said I hadn't received any messages.

I ordered a double rum and a couple of slices of lime at the bar. I squeezed the lime into the rum and then took a seat facing out into the hotel lobby. It was nearing twilight outside and people seemed in a hurry to go somewhere. Every elevator that opened into the lobby disgorged ten people or more, lots of them wearing their party finest. It occurred to me that it was almost Christmas. That didn't mean a lot to me since I don't have much of a family, nor many people in my life on whom I might lavish gifts of the season. Christmas for me was nothing more than a time of year when work tended to take a lull.

As I watched one gaggle of American tourists push through the revolving doors of the hotel, I became aware that a man had settled in the chair next to me. He was about a head shorter than I, wiry and swarthy, his hair starting to gray at the temples. He wore an expensive suit and a heavy gold ring on the third finger of his right hand.

"Guess I didn't get my invitation to the party," I said, as I took a sip of my drink and tipped the glass toward the partiers walking out the door.

"You really wanna be in the same room with those assholes?"

I turned again to face him.

"You Loame?" he asked.

"Yes. You're the courier from Miami?"

One side of his mouth turned upward and a sound like steam escaping came from it. "No. That guy waited around for you at the Riviera until one of Lansky's boys told him you'd been hustled off to the Sans Souci. So he went there and was told you never even checked in. You're a hard guy to track down."

"The Sans Souci is a little off the beaten track. The cab fees alone would have been more than Mr. Hacker's other bills combined. You work for Mr. Hacker?"

"I work for Mr. Trafficante. My name's Louis Braga."

He extended a corded hand. I shook it, surprised at the strength he had for a man his size and build. Guess you can't tell, sometimes.

"My friends call me Lucho," he added.

"Cormac Loame. Mac."

"That's okay, Mr. Loame. Mr. Trafficante don't like me getting too familiar with the contract workers."

Contract workers. Given Mr. Trafficante's line of work, that term could mean any number of things.

Braga pulled a brown envelope from his jacket pocket.

"The guy from Miami gave this to Mr.

Trafficante, who asked me to figure out where in hell you were. You were expecting this?"

I opened the envelope. Inside was a sheaf of photographs of a man whom I presumed to be Danny McCarl. He looked younger than I had expected, not much more than a teenager — though Hacker had said he was in his middle twenties — with clear blue eyes and a Troy Donohue head of blond hair. He would stand out in Havana like a two-headed Viking. That worried me. How was it nobody had noticed a guy like this dragging around a fourteen-year-old girl who looked like Veronica Lake?

"Yeah. I was expecting this. Don't suppose you've seen this guy around," I said, showing him one of the photos.

"As a matter of fact, I have seen this man. Just not recently."

"When?"

"Could have been five months ago. There was a couple of boys down here that needed to go back to the States, but they didn't seem to be in much of a hurry to get. Mr. Trafficante called up to Miami for a little assistance. Three or four other guys came down the next day and *escorted* these boys back home. This guy in the picture was one of the guys from Miami who came down."

"You're sure?"

"Why would I lie? As I recall, the kid was good with his hands. Quick and strong. So you think this guy is in Havana again?"

"Or somewhere else in Cuba. The information I got from Mr. Hacker is that this man came here several days ago with the girl."

"Shouldn't be hard to find. If you want, I'll take one of those pictures and ask around a little."

"You'd do that?"

"Mr. Trafficante wants this business over and done. Things are getting messy here in Cuba. There's talk we're all gonna have to bug out if the reds march into town. Mr. Trafficante's trying to find some safe harbors for some of his investments. With Mr. Hacker preoccupied over this business with his daughter, and with some other problems he's got up in Miami, he can't give Mr. Trafficante's problems the attention they deserve. Mr. Trafficante figures the sooner this girl of Hacker's gets back home, the better for everyone."

I told him to keep the picture. He was a local, probably knew places in town where McCarl might have visited. It would take me months to reach those places, going from bar to bar and one hotel to another.

"Thanks," I said. "Tomorrow I have to hit the bricks. It's going to be a long, tough day, so I'm turning in. If you happen to get any information, leave it with the desk clerk. I'll get it when I get back."

"So you aren't gonna do any more hotel hopping?" Braga asked. "That's good news for me. Took me almost half a day to track you down."

He pulled a card from his jacket pocket. It had a telephone number printed on it and nothing else.

"You need anything, you call that number and ask for *Lucho.* If I'm not there, leave a message and I'll meet with you in an hour or so. Mr. Trafficante wants me to take good care of you."

Chapter Fourteen

The next day, I hit every hotel, restaurant, juke joint, rum mill and taxi stand I could find in a ten-block radius of the Hilton. Everyone thought Danny McCarl looked like Troy Donohue. Nobody had seen him. Everyone thought Lila Hacker looked like Veronica Lake. Nobody had seen her. On the off chance that something nasty had happened to them, I even dropped in at the local hospitals. All I got for my day of work was sore feet and a growing distaste for everything Cuban.

About a half hour after sunset I dragged my tired body back into the Hilton and grabbed a seat at the bar. The guy behind it took my order for a cold beer. I set my hat on the mahogany and wiped at my face with my handkerchief. The Buick Roadmaster was starting to feel more distant every minute. I began to wonder whether Cecil Hacker had gotten bad information. For all

I knew, McCarl and his daughter weren't anywhere near Cuba. The Caribbean is a big place with lots of islands. McCarl might have been smarter than Hacker credited him. He could have spread the word about hitting Havana, and then headed for parts unknown with the girl.

Time was running out. As I'd tramped from one bar to the next, I'd caught bits and pieces of news from the revolution. It seemed that red forces commanded by Camilo Cienfuegos had launched an attack on a garrison at Yaguajay, and Che was starting an assault on Santa Clara. Santa Clara was only eighty miles from Havana. If it fell, there was nothing between the rebels and Batista but jungle and sugar plantations. The reds would march on the city like an army of avenging ants.

It was strange. Havana was teetering on the edge of a coup, but the people on the streets went about their business as if nothing was wrong. On the surface, nobody seemed terribly concerned that their whole way of life might be about to change. I couldn't get my head around it. Maybe they were so desperate to stay alive from one day to the next that geopolitical concerns didn't factor into their consciousness. It reminded me of the way I was back in college, when

Hitler and his cronies were not much more than obscure names in the newspaper. I had learned the hard way. I wondered how tough the lesson would be on the seemingly unsuspecting *Habaneros* on the sidewalks.

The television over the bar was tuned to CMQ. A tense-looking newscaster read from the paper he held, and I was able to gather — with my rusty Spanish — that he was still spouting the government line, that "a rout of the rebels was imminent."

Something in his eyes told me he didn't believe a word of it.

Jaime Guzman slid onto the seat next to me.

"You have been moving around," he said.

"Got a tail on me?"

"You are not that important. I had to look for you."

He slipped something heavy into my jacket pocket, and then gestured for the barkeep. I checked the pocket and found my pistol.

"Told you I didn't shoot him," I said.

"I never doubted you."

He ordered a Coca-Cola with lime, and twisted around to look directly at me so that we didn't have to carry on a conversation in the mirror.

"You doubted me enough to check my

gun," I said.

"One would not wish to lose a murderer because one did not check out the easy suspects. It would be embarrassing. I take it you haven't found your little girl."

The last bit he'd said with something like a smirk.

"If I had, I'd already be back in Miami. It's getting a little uncomfortable here." I nodded at the television screen.

"Yes. People are worried. I myself have heard that flights out of the airport are being double booked. Have you ever heard such a thing? How can you sell a seat on a plane twice?"

"Everyone wants to turn a buck if things go south. Once Fidel and his buddies roll into Havana, there will only be so many flights out before they shut down the airport. The people left behind will have more to worry about than airline refunds."

"This would be a good time for you to use your return ticket."

I took a long drag from my beer and ordered another. "You trying to get rid of me, Jaime?"

"I am thinking only of your safety. As poorly as your government regards the current government in Cuba, they would vastly prefer it over that of the rebels." He looked around, as if expecting to find someone eavesdropping. "That is, *if* they should prevail in their revolution. Should the revolution succeed, the revolutionaries might not be happy to find *yanquis.* Better to leave now, while it's safe."

"I hear you. Believe it or not, I'd leave in a minute if I could. I need to find the girl first. You haven't heard anything of her, have you?"

"No. I've had larger matters on my mind. Something else you may want to know — old Escobar has died."

I took a salutary swig from my fresh beer. "Might be the luckiest guy in town," I said.

As soon as I got back up to my room, I shed my clothes and stood in a cool shower for ten minutes, letting the water wash away sweat and grime.

The next day was Christmas Eve. In most of the United States — hell, most of the world — people were getting ready for the holiday. Children awakened each morning wringing their hands, wondering what Santa was going to bring them. Mothers slaved in kitchens making cookies and cakes for their family celebration. Schoolteachers, happy for their first break since Labor Day, decorated their meager apartments in anticipation of the New Year.

Me? I had nobody to wrap presents for and my Christmas tree was a foot-and-a-half-high celluloid thing I kept in a closet and trotted out a couple of days before the twenty-fifth so I wouldn't feel like some kind of Scrooge.

Except that, this year, there was a good chance I'd spend Christmas in a hotel bar, listening to a mambo band play *Sleigh Ride* with maracas and drowning my loneliness with Cuba Libres.

After a quarter hour under the water I finally felt clean. I dried myself with the towel, and then wrapped it around my waist before stepping out of the steamy bathroom into my air-conditioned room.

As I ran a coarse horsehair brush through my crew cut, someone knocked on my door. Nobody had telephoned the room and I wasn't expecting visitors. I grabbed Hemingway's revolver and stood to one side of the jamb.

"Who is it?" I called out, trying to sound friendly.

From the other side, I heard a plaintive female voice that I recognized immediately. I unlocked the door and opened it. "Is someone publishing my whereabouts, Marisol?" I asked, as she slid into the room and shut the door before I could get to it. "I've been in three hotels over the last two days. How'd you find me?"

She glanced at the floor and then my body, as I stood there in the hotel towel. I thought I saw something like distant interest, but I could also see she was otherwise preoccupied.

"I needed to talk to you," she said. "I started at the Riviera, but they told me you had left. I thought . . . I *hoped* you had returned to Miami."

"I'm not finished here."

"I called hotels until I found you at the Hilton."

I grabbed my shorts, pants and undershirt, and walked toward the bathroom. "Keep talking while I dress."

I left the door cracked.

"I have been hearing things," she said. "As I told you, Hector is close to Batista. There was a meeting last week between Batista and a representative of your country. The United States has deserted us to the rebels."

"I know. I heard it on one of the rebel radio stations."

"It is a matter of time, now. Fulgencio is forcing the state radio and television stations to broadcast news that makes it sound as if the government is defeating the rebels, but they are not. The battles are all going badly for the army."

I returned to the bedroom. I had changed clothes, but I still carried the revolver.

"Do you need that?" she asked. "It makes me nervous."

I opened the top drawer of the dresser, slid the revolver underneath some socks, and slipped my own automatic into the shoulder holster, which I then draped over the back of the chair.

"Why are you here?" I asked.

"I was troubled when I saw you in the Riviera the other evening. You said awful things. At first I was very angry at you."

"I don't like coincidences."

"But that's exactly what our meeting was. Hector and I had attended a dinner meeting in the hotel. He wanted to talk business in one of the lounges. I was bored. I went to the bar for a drink, and there you were."

"Just like that?"

"You sound so suspicious."

"Every mobster in Cuba seems to know I'm here. Batista's in bed with the mob — Lansky, Trafficante, the whole bunch of them. Any crook with a million dollars can open a hotel and a casino here, and it's unregulated. This place is a gold mine for lowlifes. From what you say, Hector is deep inside the organization. Are you surprised that I'm suspicious?"

She sat in the only chair in the room, leaned forward and wrung her hands as she stared at the floor. The top of her dress billowed open and for an instant I could spy the umber cleavage of her breasts, standing out starkly against her white brassiere. I felt cheap and adolescent, so I glanced away.

"No," she said. "I'm sorry. You are right."

"You didn't answer my question. Why are you here?"

"Are you interrogating me?"

Something wasn't right. I felt an electric current run up my back. She shouldn't have been here. Maybe she told the truth. Maybe she had called from hotel to hotel, searching for me. Why, though? Why all the effort to find me? Why become evasive when I asked her for reasons?

"You'd better go," I said, as I reached for the doorknob. "It could mean big trouble for you if Hector discovered you'd visited me."

"No! Please don't make me leave."

"Give me a good reason."

She held up her hand. "Wait."

I waited. She seemed to gather herself a little, her breath coming in catches. "I was heartbroken," she said. "You promised to come back for me and then I heard you had returned to Florida."

"I was shot. I had a man to take back."

"You were shot?" She raised her face to me.

"Only a little. If I had stayed in Havana, I'd have been arrested. That, and I had to take this man back to Florida for trial. I had been told to stay in Florida because it was too dangerous for me to return to Cuba to find you. You know all of this. The letters I sent —"

"I received no letters."

"I sent them. When you didn't answer, I figured you'd chosen Hector over me."

"Hector must have kept the letters from me."

"He wanted you. He hated me. Men in lust do things."

"Women, too."

"Yes. What do you want, Marisol? Why did you come here? Don't make me ask again."

She stood and gazed out the window at the Malecòn and Caribbean. "Hector and I are married, but there is no passion. I am some sort of symbol for him, a trophy. Once we were married, it was not long before his mind began to wander. He is more concerned with business and politics than he is with me. In public we pretend to be in love. I know it for the act it is. In private he no longer touches me, but I know he goes to prostitutes and to those awful sex shows. Your mobsters like to take visitors there and Hector sometimes escorts them. I went with him once —" She shuddered. "Tell me, Mac, what is going to happen after the revolution?"

"It will be bad. The rebels are reds. They'll nationalize everything, not just the government. Sugar, rum, cigars, anything they can touch. Hector will lose his farms, his restaurants, everything. Aristocrats will either escape or go up against the wall. Batista's closest advisors are dead men walking, unless they can get out. You see what's happened in Eastern Europe? It'll be like that here."

"What will become of us?"

I thought about it. "You'll survive, or you'll get steamrolled."

She rose from the chair and crossed the room. As she stopped inches from my chest, she kicked off her heels. I had forgotten how small she was in her bare feet. Her face fell against my chest.

"Since I saw you two nights ago, I haven't been able to get you out of my head," she said. "That's why I searched for you. Years have gone by, and I didn't know whether you were dead or alive. Then I saw your face in the bar, and I felt the same way I did six years ago. Is it too late, Mac? Has our time passed?"

I grasped her shoulders and held her away from me an inch or two. "You're a married woman."

"To the wrong man."

"That was your choice. Right or wrong, you decided on Hector. We can't change that, even if you wanted to."

She fell into my arms, which — in defiance of my will — folded around her.

"I do want to, Mac," she said. "I would go back and change everything. What am I going to do?"

We figured out something.

Chapter Fifteen

Sometime during the night, the electricity went off. The air conditioner stopped its drone and the silence woke me.

Marisol lay where she had fallen asleep, next to me on the bed, her hair splayed out across her pillow like a flow of spring water over silken river rocks. Without the cool air, the room grew warm quickly. A sheen of perspiration began to form on her perfect skin.

Her arm rested on my belly. I gently pushed it aside, and got out of the bed to open the window. As soon as I slid up the sash, a breeze from the Caribbean flowed into the room, rustling the sheers on the windows. It brought with it a briny aroma that I had always associated with Havana.

I glanced back at Marisol, who was still breathing softly and deeply, and allowed the thousand and one recriminations I had forestalled to flood through my brain. I never should have allowed it to happen. I knew, in retrospect, that sleeping with Marisol had opened doors that I would not be able to close again. There was Hector to deal with, for one thing. If he found out I had made love to his wife, he'd put aside Batista, the revolution, even his own propensity to punish me. If he had hated me before, he now had ample reason to detest me.

On one level I couldn't blame him.

Marisol rolled over and her eyes tried to focus on me as I stood by the window.

"It's warm," she said.

"Power's off."

"The air is nice. I like the smell."

"You shouldn't have come."

"You have regrets?"

"Boxes of them. You're only the most recent. This was wrong, Marisol. You shouldn't have come and I shouldn't have let you stay. Everything is changed now."

"How do you mean?"

I lit a cigarette and blew the smoke out the window. "What does Hector plan to do?"

"About what?"

"About Castro and Guevara. When the rebels hit Havana. Is he planning to stay or run?"

She drew the sheets around her and sat up in the bed. “Hector doesn’t believe it will come to that. He’s proud. He thinks Fulgencio’s army will beat back the rebels at the last minute.”

“He’s deluded.”

“This is our home, Mac. We have lived here all our lives. We need to believe our home will be here for us.”

I took another drag from the cigarette, but it burned my lungs. Nothing ever seemed to go right in Havana. I stubbed it out on the sill, tossed it out the window, and watched it drop toward the street. “Why in hell did you marry him?”

“What were my options? I had no reason to believe that you would return.” She fumbled with the sheets. “He was *relentless*. It was as if he saw me as some sort of prize. Hector is accustomed to getting what he wants. He wanted me. It did not matter to him that I was still in love with you. His ego blinded him to anything but his personal ambition. There is only so much of that I could withstand.”

“He wore you down.”

“Yes. In the end I think I married him to get him out of my hair.”

“How’s that working for you?”

“I’m here, am I not?”

"We have to get you out," I said. "I want you to come back to Florida with me. The man I'm working for here is connected. He works for Santo Trafficante. I can ask for favors. I can pull some strings."

I thought about the card Braga had given me, which was in my pants pocket. I wondered how far Trafficante would go to grant me a favor. Probably depended on how badly he wanted me out of the country.

"Leave my home? My family?"

"You haven't been listening. If Hector stays, he's going to die. If you stay, you might die. If you live, it won't be the way you've known all your life. Better to go to Florida and wait things out. Even if Castro and Guevara and Cienfuegos take Cuba, it'll be another thing to hang on to it. These banana republics have a short shelf life."

She closed her eyes, as if trying to imagine the shape her world would take in such a case. Then she opened her eyes and shook her head. Maybe she couldn't envision it, or maybe she wanted the images to disappear.

"What about the girl you came here to find?" she asked.

"I said *you'd* go to Florida. I still have a job to do."

She left the bed and padded over to me. The moonlight reflected off the Caribbean, making her skin seem to glow in the darkened room. For a moment I thought my heart might stop. She wrapped her arms around me and drew my mouth down to hers. We kissed for what seemed like hours. Then she pulled her head back.

"I won't leave, Mac. Not yet. Perhaps you're wrong about the rebels. They may not win."

"If they take Havana, there may not be much time to escape."

"We will deal with that when it happens."

I allowed her body to flow into mine and we stood in the moonlight, ten stories over the Malecòn, and waited for something to force us apart.

Sometime later that night, the power came back on and the air conditioner started again.

I was awakened around eight-thirty by the jangling of the telephone next to the bed. Reflexively, I jerked my hand out and grabbed the receiver.

"Mac!" Rico called from the other end. "You are a naughty man!"

I felt a flash of panic. What did Rico know? What might he have told Hector? I heard the shower running in the bathroom and under the spray of water I could make out

Marisol's voice, humming a slow island song.

"You might want to explain that," I said, hoping my voice didn't quaver.

"You turn down my hospitality and then you disappear from your hotel. It took me two days to find you. One might think you are in hiding!"

"I was forced to move out of the Riviera. It's a long story. I've been busy scouring Havana for the missing girl."

"I'm sure this is a story I would like to hear. Why don't we have breakfast and discuss it?"

The water had stopped during the brief exchange. The bathroom door opened and Marisol stepped out into the room, wearing a towel wrapped around her waist. She started to ask me who was on the telephone. I covered the microphone and silently mouthed *your brother-in-law.*

She looked stricken. I shook my head and pointed to the chair to suggest that she sit down.

"Breakfast might be nice, Rico, but not here in the hotel," I said. "I'm sick of hotel food. What about that place we went to the other day? Hector's restaurant?"

"I have a better idea. There is a small place I like. You know La Bodeguita del Medio?"

"It's on Empedrado, right? They don't serve breakfast, or at least they didn't six years ago."

"That's the beauty of it, Mac! We will be alone. Nobody but you, me, and our business."

"What business is that?"

He laughed. "The business that brought you to Havana. I have some news for you. Shall we meet at — say, nine-thirty? Will that give you time to hustle your little barmaid out and clean yourself up?"

"No hustling needed, Rico. I'm by myself. The Bodeguita, nine-thirty."

"Breakfast is on you and your fabulous Mafia expense account. Believe me, it will be worth it!"

He hung up and I stared at the receiver in my hand.

"What did he want?" Marisol asked from the chair.

"Breakfast. He implied that he knows something about the girl I'm chasing. Get dressed. I'm going to shower and shave. It would be better if I leave first, and you stay here for about a half hour. When you don't hear anyone in the hallway, maids included, you can go. The last thing I need right now is for some nosy hotel dick to find you leaving my room and have word get back to

Hector."

She crossed the room and settled next to me on the bed. The view of her breasts stole my breath.

"You will be careful," she said, after kissing me. "I want to see you tonight."

"Too risky. Let me find out what Rico knows. If I can get a line on the girl, I can find her and arrange to leave the country. If I do, you're coming with me, understand?"

I saw the tears form in her eyes. They nearly broke what heart I had left.

Chapter Sixteen

The Calle Empedrado was a fixture in Habana Vieja, or the old quarter of the city. The streets were cobblestone, and the city had embedded cannonballs in the pavement to keep cars from driving down the single-lane passages. The buildings were some of the oldest on the island, dating back to the colonial times when the island was as likely to be ravaged by pirates as by hurricanes. There was a mix of the pastel stucco you see everywhere in the Caribbean, and stone structures intended to withstand the onslaught of eight-pound balls fired from the harbor.

You enter Empedrado by way of the Plaza de la Catedral, where the Palacio de los Marqueses de Aguas Claras is marked by two-story-high sandstone arches supported by columns. From there, the road narrows, and the sidewalks have to be walked single-file. It's not a place you want to wander late at night, because after the bars and the restaurants close, the streets are claimed by people who find the scales balancing your life and your wallet tipped strongly toward leather. Wander down the wrong alley off the Empedrado in the dark, and you could be killed for your shoes.

It's a safe enough place in the daytime, though, if you don't mind sidestepping beggars and pickpockets on the way to your destination, which in my case was La Bodeguita del Medio. I dodged a suspicious pool of liquid on the curb as I stepped into the restaurant.

It was dark inside and cooler than on the street. Like many structures in the islands, the interior had high ceilings, designed to trap the heat of the day. The walls were thick plaster with thousands of little bits of graffiti, captured moments by tourists wishing to leave their mark on Cuba before tramping back to their sedate American lives. Archways were supported by wooden beams, and a second level was delineated by strong mahogany balusters. There were framed photos everywhere, some dating back to the days of the rum wars in the Roaring Twenties — famous actors and singers and gangsters, all of them sitting at Bodeguita tables grinning from too many daiquiris and too much *ropa vieja.*

It took my eyes a moment to adjust to the darkness, after walking ten blocks in searing sunlight. As images began to emerge from the gloom, I saw that the place was empty. A man rounded a corner and greeted me.

"Señor Loame?"

"Yes."

"This way, please. Señor Gonzalez is waiting for you."

I followed him through several small rooms, until we reached a private booth in the rear of the restaurant. The booth was set into an alcove, with a curtain to assure privacy. We wouldn't need the curtain. Rico Gonzalez sat on one side of the booth, munching on a slice of *pan y mantequilla,* one of the Bodeguita's house specialties. When he saw the host escort me in his direction, he dropped the bread and stood, his arms outstretched.

"Mac! So nice to see you again! Please, come sit with me and we will talk about all the things we didn't have time for the other day! Would you like a drink?"

"Bloody Mary," I told the host, who then scurried off in the direction of the bar.

"Sit. Sit!" Rico urged, so I slid into the booth across from him.

"You said you had news," I said.

"Of course. We'll get to that. Here, have some bread."

He slid the basket toward me. I broke a piece off the long Cuban loaf and smeared some butter on it, glad he had offered since I hadn't eaten dinner the night before — being otherwise occupied with his sister-in-law — and my stomach was clenching. I didn't want to guzzle a Bloody Mary on an empty stomach.

"I took the liberty of ordering for us," Rico said between bites. *"Ceviche de camarones* and *tortillas* with *café con leche."*

"Sounds good. Look, Rico, I'm sorry about ditching you the other day."

"Think nothing of it. I had taken a *pelota* to the head, Mac. I was not in my right mind. I was *loco.* The rum made me evil and I said things I did not mean. It is I who should apologize. And, so, here we are."

I tried to suppress my own guilt feelings over the fact that I had for all intents and purposes taken him up on his suggestion that I "finish what I had started so many years ago" with Marisol.

The waiter brought my drink, along with two large wine glasses filled with the *ceviches de camarones* — shrimp cured in-house, and served with lime juice, coconut milk, black beans, cilantro and mild peppers. That was one of the things that had always surprised me about Cuba. Unlike most Latin cultures, the food in Havana was never over-spicy. Instead, the Cubanos depended on blending contrasting flavors to tease and torture the palate, without frying it beyond sensation.

"I will return with your tortillas shortly," the waiter said. "Enjoy, please, señores."

Rico waited for me to take a bite or two of the *camarones.* They were delicious, as I had expected.

"You should be honored," he said. "La Bodeguita usually does not open until noon, and then only for drinking and lunch. I persuaded the owner to allow us to meet here for breakfast."

"Must have cost you a bundle."

"Between you and me? The owner is afraid of my brother. He tried to cheat me, but I mentioned Hector's name and he cut his price in half. Shrewd, eh?"

He grinned at me, white teeth like ivory gravestones flashing in the light from the overhead chandeliers.

"Nobody can fault you for your business sense," I replied. "Which, as I recall, is why we're meeting. You have some news for me?"

"It will hold. I'm in no rush, and I don't wish to speak of such matters and spoil my appetite. We will discuss it over *café con leche* in a bit. You will see. It will be worth the wait."

The waiter returned in a few moments to clear away the *ceviche* glasses and replace them with plates of *tortillas.* Unlike Mexican tortillas, these were similar to crepes and filled with fried onions, potatoes and chopped *chorizo* sausage. It was Cuba's version of the Spanish omelet. The *ceviche* had quieted the rumble in my stomach, but I knew it was only temporary. The *tortillas* would keep it contented for a while.

As we ate, we talked about jai alai and the rebels and American baseball, but I could tell Rico was amped up to spill some sort of huge secret he hoarded. I was too distracted by the *tortillas* to push him. It seemed like ages since I had forced down a few *empanadas* in a dive off the Prado while wearing out my shoes on the pavement the day before. I hoped it didn't look as if I was gobbling.

Finally, we finished, and the waiter brought *café con leche,* coffee with hot milk and enough raw turbinado sugar to etch your teeth, and a *tostada* — a loaf of toasted Cuban bread with thick butter on the side.

Following Rico's lead, I slathered a slice of bread with the butter, and dipped it in the coffee. A skim of fat formed on the coffee's surface and quickly evacuated to the rim of the cup. I had forgotten about this little slice of heaven. I took the first bite and almost involuntarily closed my eyes to savor it.

Rico interrupted my reverie. "How much is your girl worth to you?" he asked.

I settled back in the booth. "That depends. What do you have for me?"

He smiled and took a sip of his coffee. "Your first problem is that you are not from Cuba. Your second problem is that you don't have the social connections I enjoy. I showed the picture you gave me around, in places you can't go, and I had a line on the girl within a couple of hours. I made a few telephone calls and met with her last night."

"You saw her?"

"In the flesh. I must say, Mac, her picture does not do her justice. Had I not known she is only fourteen, I think I might have sampled a little of that *yanqui bollo.*"

I knew the word *bollo.* It wasn't complimentary.

"You're becoming crude again, Rico. She's a kid."

"As I reminded myself repeatedly."

"Was McCarl with her? Guy about six feet tall, blond hair, wears it a little long?"

"He was the other reason I did not make a move on her. He hovered over her like an angry mosquito. I considered having him dropped from an airplane, but she seemed to like him, so . . ." He shrugged.

"He had a gun on you."

"That also factored into my decision. I told the girl there was a man in Havana looking for her, and that I could arrange for you and her to be brought together. I am sad to say that she declined."

"So you let her go?"

"Not precisely. I know where you can find the little one. There are eyes watching her, so that brings us back to the original question. How much is she worth to you?"

"Her father has considerable resources. He'll pay whatever you ask."

Rico pushed his coffee cup to the middle of the table. "That is good, Mac. You see, I have considerable needs. This revolution business is troubling. Hector sucks incessantly at Fulgencio's . . . tit — you see, sometimes I can exercise restraint. Hector believes whatever Batista feeds him, but I see things more clearly. I understand that, soon, many of us may need to make a short trip across the Florida Straits. We may not have a lot of time to pack. I would like to know I have a livelihood waiting for me when I get wherever I am going. Do we understand each other?"

"You think you're going to have to blow to Florida and you need a stake."

"Good. We are of one mind, I see. Hector, being first born, controls all the Gonzalez fortune. I live on a generous allowance and from money I make betting on jai alai, but if the rebels take over the country I cannot depend on that to continue. Now, if I had, say, a hundred thousand *yanqui* dollars in an American bank in Miami, my head would rest much more easily at night.

"Cuban *pesos* won't be worth wiping your ass after the revolution," he continued. "I need a currency that is more stable. Dollars seem like a nice choice, considering that I plan to live in your country. You and me, we can hang out together more often. You'd like that, wouldn't you?"

"Of course. How do I know you have access to the girl, though? Mr. Hacker is going to want assurances."

Rico slipped his hand into his jacket pocket and pulled out a Polaroid photo, which he slid across the table to me. In it, he sat at a glass-topped wicker table with a woman whose flaxen hair swept across half her face. I could plainly see that she was Lila Hacker. She sipped a daiquiri through a straw and sat close to Rico. He held a copy of the previous day's Havana newspaper, *Prensa Libre,* so I'd know the picture was recent. Behind Lila Hacker was the torso of a man dressed in what appeared to be American clothes — wool trousers no sane person would wear in Cuba and a tweed sport coat over a white shirt. The top of the photo cut off his face, but I figured him for Danny McCarl.

"She tells an interesting story," Rico said. "I think it is one you will want to hear."

"Why?"

"You might not be so eager to return her to Miami once you have spoken with her."

"A job's a job," I said, as I finished my coffee. "One way or another, she goes back to Florida. What happens after that doesn't concern me."

"What happened before she fled Florida might."

"I doubt it. You want a hundred grand for the girl? I need to be sure you can deliver."

"She isn't going anywhere. I have a number of eyes on her. She cannot take a piss without me knowing."

I reached for my hat. "I'll contact Mr. Hacker and let him know about your offer, and I'll get back to you soon. Do you already have a stateside bank account?"

"Yes. I'll provide you with the information as soon as Mr. Hacker agrees."

I dropped a handful of Cuban pesos on the table to cover breakfast and stepped back out of La Bodeguita del Medio into the Calle Empedrado. It was close to noon and the streets were bustling with Christmas Eve traffic. Sidewalk vendors hoping to score last-minute gift sales sat in the shade and guarded their wares. A couple of them saw me leave the restaurant and tried to draw me in with head nods and hand gestures. I ignored them.

Rico might have been right. I wasn't from Cuba and I didn't enjoy his social connections. But what he had not considered was that I wasn't stupid, either. Being a child of privilege, Rico had been raised with a sense of entitlement and a disregard for the lower classes. However we might have taken pleasure in each other's company — at least at one time — it would have been foolhardy to think he regarded me as anything other than hired help, below his social caste.

I was of the opinion that he expected me to dash straight to my hotel, or even the nearest Western Union office, and pass his offer on to Cecil Hacker. If I was just a dumb hired gumshoe, I would have done that. Rico was my connection to Lila and

McCarl, though, and I wasn't about to let him out of my sight.

As I left La Bodeguita, I turned left, toward the water, instead of right toward the Plaza de la Catedral. About half a block from the entrance to the restaurant, I took cover behind a column, and watched for Rico to leave.

After five or ten minutes, I started to worry that he had accessed a rear door. I was about to leave my cover and head back toward the restaurant when he stepped from the doorway and turned toward the cathedral. I blended in with the sparse parade of Empedrado tourists, about fifty yards behind him. If he suspected I was in the area, he did a good job of hiding it, because he kept strolling toward the Palacio de los Marqueses de Aguas Claras. When he reached Avenue del Misiones, he hailed a taxi.

I was a little surprised that he moved about alone. First, he was something of a public figure, being the famous Ricky Gonzalez of the Fronton Jai Alai. Also, he was the brother of an important member of Batista's core disciples. It occurred to me that he might have slipped his own protective forces — if he had them — in order to meet with me. Was he heading back to their shield, or to contact Lila Hacker to tell her about our meeting?

I whistled for a cab, and climbed in behind the driver. I did a quick translation from English into my doubtful Spanish and pointed at Rico's cab.

"I think the man in that taxi is fucking my wife. I need to know where he is going. Follow him, but stay back two hundred feet or so."

Machismo was as healthy in Havana as in any Hispanic country, and the hack driver was only too willing to comply. He put the car in gear and peeled away from the curb.

"You catch this man with your *esposa,* what you do with him?" he asked, as he glanced toward me in the backseat. He said it in English, which told me that my Spanish still needed a lot of work.

I pulled my jacket away, and showed him the .38 in my shoulder holster. Nobody loves the prospect of seeing some wife-stealing crumb take a bullet more than a Habanero. I felt the cab lurch forward as he stabbed the loud pedal. Within seconds we were situated in traffic five car lengths behind Rico. We stayed there as he traveled around the traffic circle at Via Monumental, the start of the Malecòn. Instead of taking the waterfront highway, he doubled back on the Calle de Prado, going the opposite direction from where he'd come. I couldn't figure that out. He could have cut across on Neptuno, or Animas, or Trocadero if he wanted to hit the Prado. Why had he gone all the way to the water?

Perhaps, I thought, he had planned to take the Malecòn, but at the last second changed his mind. That could have meant he had made me. If that was the case, I could probably follow him all day. The only way to be sure was to stay behind and see if he stopped somewhere.

A block past Dragones, we hit another traffic circle, where Rico headed off on Maximo Gomez. I told the cabbie to stay several cars back.

Tailing someone is a labor-intensive process, if you don't want to get famous doing it. Back in Miami, when I had time to plan it, I would sometimes day-hire another PI or two to help me set up a decent tail. That way, we could take turns following the mark, to avoid detection. If you're trying to bird-dog some guy alone, it helps to have an intimate familiarity with the surface streets, so that you could occasionally turn off, run parallel for a couple of intersections, and then fall back in behind him. If he thought he was being followed, that might throw him off.

My memory of Havana streets was flimsy at best. If I told my driver to turn left or right, I could be halfway back to Florida before I knew it, and I would have lost Rico. Clearly, I was at the disadvantage in this pursuit.

I was about to ask the driver whether there was a good parallel street we could briefly access, when Rico's cab pulled over to the curb along the Avenue Arroyo. I told my driver to do the same. Rico hopped from his cab and started hoofing it up the street.

I handed some bills to the cabbie and he looked at them reluctantly.

"You want, señor, I drive up alongside him and you can —" He pointed his index finger like a gun and made *bang* noises. "You want, no charge for the ride."

This cabbie was an action freak. He wanted to see Rico take one for the team.

"Not this time, *amigo,*" I told him. "I'm still not certain he's the one."

The driver shrugged and scooped up the money as I opened the door and stepped out onto the shell-and-cement sidewalk. The cab had been hot, but at least the air in it had been moving. On the street the heat slapped at me like an angry mistress and almost took my breath away. Fifteen years in the tropics and it still got to me.

As my taxi pulled away from the curb, I saw Rico about two hundred feet in front of me, walking quickly, facing down, shoulders slumped. He looked like someone with a problem and a destination.

He turned abruptly at an ancient stone church, scrambled up the steps, and entered through the right side of a pair of twenty-foot-high wooden doors. I noted on the sign outside that it was the Iglesia del Sante Francisco. The fact that it was called an *iglesia* instead of a *catedral* indicated its size. Why Rico might have sought such a place confounded me. He had mentioned many times his distaste for all things spiritual.

Of course, people can change, despite the fact that, in Rico's case, the likelihood was pretty slim.

I waited a moment to see if he might be trying to catch me following, and then I stepped up to the doors and entered the church.

Inside, it was dark and cool and there was a strange scent that seemed a mélange of spicy incense and mold. I quickly slid to the side, behind a second doorway, while I allowed my eyes to adjust to the limited light.

It took a couple of minutes, but after I could see better I chanced a quick once-over. It was a typical Caribbean Catholic church, with shrines set around the outer walls of the nave. Instead of statues of patron saints, the shrines were marked by tapestries depicting the saints in the course of performing one miracle or another. In front of the tapestries were stepped tables with votive candles for those making special prayers. At that moment it didn't sound like such a bad idea.

As my vision sharpened in the gloom, I began to scan the nave, looking for Rico. There were only five or six people scattered around the room, most of them on kneelers, their hands clasped around rosaries as they performed penances. None of them looked like Rico, but all I could see was the back of heads. I couldn't see into the transepts, and for all I knew he might have ducked into one of them and was waiting there with a nasty surprise for me should I stick my head around the corner.

I was about to commit to stepping into the nave from the narthex, when I felt something hard and cold press against the back of my neck.

"Don't turn around," someone said.

"No problem."

"You followed Gonzalez?"

"Yeah."

"That was a bad idea."

"You know, I was just thinking the same thing."

I could tell immediately that he was an American. His voice was resonant, his accent flat, like someone from the middle of the United States. He sounded like the kind of guy who grew up with endless vistas and not a lot of people crowding them, the kind of kid who had raised a calf for 4-H and had parents with names like Boyd and Judy, and who had somehow managed to make some bad decisions in the intervening years.

"McCarl?"

The object in the back of my neck pressed harder.

"Don't be stupid," he said. "I haven't decided yet whether you're walking out of here."

"Do I get a vote?"

"That depends on what you're here for."

"You'd shoot me in a church?"

"A church, a bar, a hotel, it's all pretty much the same to me. I don't want to kill you, but having you here complicates my life and I haven't figured out what to do about that yet."

"You give it a lot of thought," I said. "Take your time."

"How long since your last confession?"

It was a strange question, but I decided to

play along. "Never. I'm not Catholic."

"Seems like a good time to take it up. When I tell you, walk over to the confessional and sit in the left chamber. Don't do anything crazy. I'll have the gun on you the whole time, and if you try to alert anyone, I won't mind using it."

"How long do I sit there? Long enough for you to bolt, I suppose."

"Don't put thoughts in my head. I'm making this up as I go along. Move."

I entered the nave and wended my way around the back of the pews toward the confessional. When I reached it, I glanced back at the narthex then pointed toward the left chamber. The shadowy figure nodded, so I pulled open the door and stepped inside.

If I had thought the nave was murky, the confessional was downright dismal. It smelled like dust and sweat and years of mortal fear and desperate pleading for absolution, with a touch of mildew. I'm not normally claustrophobic — or *anything*-phobic, for that matter — but as I sat in the dark, waiting for either some indication I could leave or a barrage of bullets, I began to feel clammy.

Since I had no idea what would happen next, and because I've always felt braver with a firearm handy, I pulled the automatic from my shoulder holster, thumbed the hammer, and laid it on my thigh. I was ready for action should the need arise. And if I had a chance to respond to it.

After about five minutes, the window between the chambers slid open. I could glimpse a dark figure on the other side of the lattice and I could hear breathing. Beyond that, the other person might have been Santa Claus, for all I knew.

He said nothing for several moments. Instead, he sat on the other side of the screen and breathed like an asthmatic. I was probably wheezing a little myself.

"Father?" I asked, tentatively, when the silence between us grew too overwhelming.

"I still haven't decided whether to shoot you."

"Jesus! This is a confessional!"

"Like you, I'm not a Catholic. Grew up Methodist. We don't need any stinkin' priests to intercede for us. Confessional means nothing to me. So, tell me what it is you want."

"Right now, I'd prefer not to get shot. You should know I have my own gun pointed at you. There's no way in these shadows that you can shoot me without me getting in a couple of shots of my own."

The person on the other side of the confessional didn't respond.

"I might add," I said, "that if you try to run, I'll probably go ahead and shoot anyway. Are you open to suggestions?"

A pause and then, "I'm listening."

"I'm going to suggest we both put our hardware away and talk this out without holding each other at gunpoint. I'm a reasonable man. You obviously have something you want me to understand."

I've been around guns all my life. I know the sound when a hammer is gently lowered back into place. I also noted that I didn't hear a safety click, so the guy on the other side might have backed down, but he wasn't completely committed.

"Let's start with this," I said. "You are McCarl, right?"

"Yes," he said, quietly.

"How did you know I'd follow Rico here?"

"I didn't. Rico did. He said you weren't stupid, but he wanted us to meet on neutral ground. He thought if he'd brought Lila and me to the restaurant this morning, you'd have taken her, even if it meant killing me."

"Rico has an inflated opinion of my dangerousness. He also said you and the girl have a story to tell."

"We'll get to that. How much is Madman

paying you?"

"A few grand and expenses."

"You come cheap."

"Butter me up some more. I'm having a ball here."

"Think about it, Loame. This is his daughter. The Madman is mobbed up to the knot in his tie. Trafficante owns his ass. You don't think he could contact Trafficante and have him find us down here? He didn't, though, and we knew he wouldn't. That's why we came here."

"Tell me more."

"Ask yourself why he doesn't go to Trafficante."

"Trafficante has his hands full right now. In case you haven't heard, this island is headed for a bad fall. Maybe you knew that and decided it made Cuba safe for you."

"It's not that. You know anything about the mobs, Loame?"

"A little. I've been in Miami for over a decade and a half. I've run across gangsters from time to time."

"You know about their codes? Their rules?"

"What about them?"

"There are things that are sacred. Family, for instance. These guys are businessmen, for christ's sake. They know enough not to shit where they eat. Guys like me and Hacker, we're kept around for convenience. We don't have the right guinea heritage. Our blood doesn't have the right percentage of garlic and olive oil. You understand?"

"You're not from the old country, so you don't get made."

"That's it. Hacker's nothing but a glorified money launderer. I'm some moke he pulled out of the ring on Ten-Dollar Fight Night when he realized I could take a lot of punches to the head without forgetting how to use a fork. My job is to get between Hacker and bullets should someone decide he's expendable."

"You don't think Trafficante gives a damn about Hacker."

"Oh, he gives a damn. Problem is, Hacker's got some trouble coming. The Feds are all over his books and they don't like the bottom line. You ask me, they're about to indict him for bank fraud and money laundering."

"Which could lead them back to Trafficante."

"Hell, that's where they *started.* Right now Trafficante wants to keep Hacker happy, so he won't squeal to the Feds. There's something else, though. It's that *family* thing I mentioned. You ever heard of a guy named

Frank Testaverde?"

"No."

"I heard about this from one of Trafficante's Miami guys. The Benvenuto family has run Teamster operations in central Massachusetts since six days before baseball. Seems this Testaverde guy married one of Joey Benvenuto Junior's second or third cousins, I don't know for certain. Whatever, this chick wasn't even close to the family. Anyway, Frankie had a drinking habit and a nasty temper, and some nights he'd come home and swat the missus around a few times before dragging her back to the bedroom to give it to her up the chute. I mean, according to this guy in Miami, Frank Testaverde was the stuff the stuff at the bottom of the barrel shits."

"Okay," I said, not certain where he was going.

"So, you should know that Joey Junior's not mobbed up or anything. Seems like Joe Senior wants to keep him out of the business. Joey got all upset when he heard what was happening to Testaverde's wife and he mentioned it to his dad, like he didn't know what was going to happen, right? Now, since the wife is Joey's second or third cousin, or whatever, she's also related to Joe Senior and Carmine, and Carmine . . . well, let's say Carmine has a lot stronger ties to the families than his kid brother. He starts asking around, and it isn't long before he hears from two or three other sources about Testaverde whaling on his wife and cornholing her. Family is important to these people, Loame. Testaverde wasn't even mobbed up. He was this steel worker in Pittsburgh who happened to marry a distant relation of the Benvenutos, but he was treating her with a real lack of respect. He was bringing dishonor on the family.

"Now, the Benvenutos decided to cut this guy a little slack, since they figured he didn't know who he was fooling with, so they paid him a visit and laid the whole situation out for him as clearly as they could. He was only in the hospital for a couple of days; it could've been a lot worse. What can I say? The guy was an idiot. He got better, but he brought a grudge home from the hospital and the next time he got drunk he lost control and beat his wife half to death. Except this time Benvenuto's guys in Pittsburgh were keeping an eye on him."

"Word got back to the family pretty quickly."

"They knew within the hour. Carmine Benvenuto blows up like dynamite. He's ready to hop a plane and fly down right that minute, but his dad — who always had a pretty cool head — told him to sit tight. He passed the word back channel that the gloves came off with Frank Testaverde.

"There was this bar Testaverde liked to hit on the way home from work. Some guy in the bar the next night decided to hit the head to take a leak. A few minutes later he runs out and pukes his Iron City all over a pinball machine, crying and yelling about some dead guy in the toilet. The bartender called the police and they found Testaverde with his head stuffed in a crapper, sitting in a pool of blood that came from where his dick used to be. They never found the dick. He went to his grave without his stuff. Here's my point, Loame. These people have a code, and they mean it. You don't fuck with their money or their women, even if the women are way out on a limb of the family tree."

He didn't say anything for a moment, so I decided to push the conversation along a little.

"I'd think you'd have learned a thing or two from that story," I said. "What were you thinking, stealing away to Cuba with Hacker's daughter — his *underaged* daughter at that?"

I thought I heard a sort of exasperated

gasp from the other side.

"Haven't you been listening?" McCarl said. "I didn't bring Lila here to seduce her. I brought her here to *protect* her!"

"I don't get it."

"What did Hacker tell you about Lila?"

"He said her mother had died and he had brought Lila to live with him."

"When she was ten years old."

"So?"

"She'd already spent almost all her life with her stepfather, and suddenly Cecil 'The Madman' Hacker steps up and decides he's going to be her father? Didn't you wonder why?"

"He *was* her father, after all, and he told me he never allowed the stepfather to adopt her. He had his rights."

"What about *her* rights?"

"She's a kid. Kids don't have rights."

"Jesus! For a smart guy, you sure are dense. Did you ever see a picture of Lila's mother?"

"No."

"Lila looks like her, only more . . . well, let's leave it at more. Hacker didn't want Lila *just to be his daughter.*"

Suddenly I realized what he meant. I felt nauseated and furious, all at once. "You're saying he . . . *wanted* her?"

"The same way every guy seems to want her. She's beautiful, she's smart, and let's face it, for fourteen she's got a hell of a body. I'm ashamed to say it, but that doesn't make it any less true. Lila came to me a few weeks back, crying, and she told me what her . . . what Hacker had done with her — *to* her. I almost killed him that night, but she pulled me back, begged me not to hurt him. She wanted to be with her stepfather."

"Her stepfather's in California."

"Not anymore. After Lila's mother died, he took a job with a foreign bank in Cayman Brac. The Caymans don't have extradition to the States. We've been trying to get there, to deliver her to her stepfather."

"I'm confused," I said. "What would her stepfather be doing with a bank in the Caymans? Hacker told me he was an insurance salesman."

"Hacker gets things wrong. A lot. He took too many to the head. Sometimes he stops talking in the middle of a sentence and stares off into space. Lila's stepfather is an investment banker. She'd be ten times better off with him. Why should she have to put up with some brain-damaged, mobbed-up pederast, even if he *is* her natural father?"

"Let's say this is all true," I said. "Cayman Brac isn't Cuba. Why didn't you take her there?"

"It was a matter of time. We had to get out of Miami as quickly as possible, and Havana was the first flight out. We got here, and the first night, while we were trying to figure out how to get over to the Caymans, our room was robbed. All I had after that was the money in my pocket. I've been getting by doing some short con games here and there, but it's been hand-to-mouth. Now, with the revolution, getting a plane or boat off the island takes a lot more scratch than I can produce."

It was my turn to go silent. I'd absorbed a huge amount of information in ten minutes. I needed to sort it all out.

"I need a way to contact you," I said. "I still work for Hacker. I need to tell him something, but right now I have no idea what it might be. If I find out you're telling me the truth, I need a way to get to you, work out some kind of solution."

"You think I'm stupid? I wanted to meet with you, tell you how things really are, so I could get you off our backs. I'm not interested in making any kind of deals with you, or working out any *solutions.* Soon as I can, I'm getting Lila off this island and over to Cayman Brac. I'm hoping this guy Rico can help us. I figured if you knew how things were, you'd cut us some slack."

"I have a job to do," I said.

"I'm taking my life in my hands, here, Loame! Once I get to Cayman, I can't never leave. At least, I sure can't go back to the States. I set one foot in Miami and Hacker'll turn me into gator shit. He finds out I'm anywhere in the forty-eight and I got no place to hide. The mob's everywhere. They have people in every state of the union. Why in hell would I run off with a fourteen-year-old kid with that kind of heat hanging over me, unless it was for her own good?"

"You don't have to tell me where you're hiding. Just tell me how to reach you."

Silence. I half expected him to bolt from the confessional booth. If he had, I wasn't at all certain I'd have chased him.

"Contact Rico," he said at last. "Rico knows what's going on. I think he sympathizes. You let him know you need to talk with me again, he'll set it up."

"I want to see Lila if we meet again. I need to know she's safe."

"You don't get to see her. That's not how things are going to work. You're still supposed to take her back to Hacker. I can't allow that. You deal with me, or not at all. I'm going to leave now. I'm backing out of the church. You stay here, count to a hundred, real slow. If I see you leave this booth before I'm outside, I *will* start shooting. You understand?"

"I hear you."

There was the sound of the booth door opening, and a thought suddenly occurred to me.

"McCarl!" I whispered, as loudly as I dared.

The light from the other side of the booth, which had filtered through the lattice, disappeared, and I was sure he had left.

"What?"

"I don't owe you this. Remember that. Don't trust Rico. I've known him for years. He's a great drinking buddy, but he's not trustworthy. He's lazy, he's avaricious, and right now he's a little desperate. For all you know, he may be trying to sell you to Hacker himself. He wanted a hundred thousand from me earlier today to hand Lila over. He wanted me to take the offer to Hacker. You can't depend on him."

A beat, then, "You're being straight with me?"

"I didn't have to tell you. If you're depending on Rico to protect you, you'd be wise to have a Plan B."

I thought I could make out the shadow on

the other side of the lattice nod once or twice.

"Thanks," he said. "Now I don't know who to trust."

"Probably better that way."

This time, he did leave the booth. I sat inside and counted to three hundred, to be safe. While I counted, I tried to figure out exactly how many angles this case had.

Chapter Seventeen

As I expected, Marisol was gone when I returned to my room. I did a cursory sweep for bugs — my experience at the Riviera had made me a little paranoid — and when I found none, I called the hotel operator and requested an overseas cable line to Miami. She told me there was a lot of traffic and it might take a half hour or more to clear a connection. I wasn't surprised. With the political situation what it was, I had a feeling there were a lot of negotiations going on between Cubans and their American friends.

I sat in the chair on the balcony with a cigarette, and stared out over the Malecòn at the Caribbean as I tried to analyze what I knew and what I thought I knew.

I had expected McCarl to try to scare me off the case in order to save his own hide. Instead, he had pleaded for Lila Hacker's sake. As soon as Rico had told him I was likely to tail him to the church, McCarl could have grabbed the girl and hightailed it into the mountains, where it might have taken me years to find him — as if anyone on the island had anywhere near that much time for anything.

Rico's advantage was hard to figure. On the one hand, he wanted a hundred grand to help ship Lila back to the States. On the other, he purposefully led me to McCarl, whom he knew would muddy the waters by implying Cecil Hacker's incestuous motive for retrieving his daughter. The mental image of the Madman forcing himself on Lila sickened me. I had taken money from all sorts of people over the years, for all kinds of sordid jobs. This one made me want to pack my bags, hop the next Pan Am clipper to Miami, and stuff the remainder of Hacker's advance down his throat.

I needed more information. I had thought McCarl might be some small-brained thug, but I'd found him surprisingly articulate and reasoned. It was possible he was feeding me a line, trying to divert my attention away from the girl by souring me on her father. If that were the case, he had accomplished more than half his job.

On top of all my other confusion, there was Marisol. The future she faced on the island after the insurrection, I wouldn't wish on anyone. I had to find a way to get her back to the States. In bed with her the night before, I had resolved never to abandon her again the way I had in 1952. One way or the other, we were bound to each other and Hector be damned!

The telephone rang, and the hotel operator told me my overseas line was ready. I asked for the Miami operator, and after I was connected I asked for a call to Nelson Aquilino.

Nelson was another private eye in Miami. I'd used him on occasion to help with complicated tails. He was bright, he was dependable and — most importantly — he owed me a favor.

He answered on the second ring.

"Where in hell are you, Mac? You sound like you're calling from a submarine."

"I'm in Havana. I need some help."

"I can't make it to Havana right now. It's Christmas. The kids, you know."

"I don't need you to come here. I'm working a case involving a missing girl. She might have been abducted, but it's also possible she ran away. She might have had a great reason to run. I need you to dig up some dirt on her father, if there is any."

"Sure. It's slow right now and my holiday

rates aren't so stiff."

"The girl's name is Lila Hacker. She's fourteen. Her father is Cecil Hacker."

There was a long silence on the other end, and then a sound like air seeping from a cut tire.

"The Madman?" he finally said.

"Yeah."

"He's in the papers this morning. Treasury Department's all over him. They want to pin him to the wall for, you know, the stuff he does for the bent-nose crowd."

"He's my client. He told me something about the investigation, but he didn't give me any details. But I don't think that has anything to do with the girl and she's my case."

"What do you want to know about Hacker?"

I thought for a minute. In my mind, I knew what I wanted, but putting it into words proved difficult.

"This is going to sound strange, since he's the guy paying me. I need to know what he likes in the way of girls. Specifically, does he prefer them young?"

"Young as in what? Twenty?"

"No. Younger. Think real young."

Again a long silence, interrupted only by the hum of the undersea cable. "You think he's been puttin' it to his daughter?"

Like I said, Nelson is bright. He doesn't miss a trick. "There's been an allegation. That's all I can say. The guy who brought her down here, Danny McCarl, seems to think he's protecting her from her old man. It could make a difference. If it's true, I may have to make a decision whether to bring her home."

"If it's true, you can bring her home anytime you want because I'll kill the son of a bitch myself. I got daughters, Loame."

"Don't do anything. Find out what you can and feed me the information. I'd start by talking with the owners of the clubs where he hangs out. If he's into bobby-soxers, they'll know. Pay them off well enough to keep them quiet. I don't want word to get back to Hacker that you're asking around about him. Oh, and I remember hearing through the back channels that he sometimes has parties with some of Cecille Martinez's girls. See if he asks them to — you know — dress up in schoolgirl clothes or something."

"If I'm going to talk with Cecille, I might need a lot of walking-around money."

"You remember your own daughters. If you want to hire some of Cecille's employees for one-on-one interrogations, you're doing it on your own nickel. Find out where Lila Hacker goes to school. Talk to some of her friends there. My guess is, if her father is messing with her, she hasn't kept it to herself. Her friends might be able to confirm the rumors."

"This is a hell of a thing," Nelson said. "Here at Christmas. Hey, is it as bad as they say down there? Is the whole island about to go up in smoke?"

"It's strange. There's tension, but nobody seems panicked. It's like everyone's holding their cards, waiting for someone to call the hand. If the reds get within twenty miles of the city, I expect it'll get noisy. Keep an eye on the news reports."

We talked some more about Cuba and Cecil Hacker and what could happen if the reds did take over the island, but I was paying international cable rates by the minute so it was a short conversation.

I was out of ideas. In one sense I had located Hacker's daughter, or at least I knew how to get with her if I needed to. The real question now was whether to grab her and dash back to Miami, or wait and see how the information boiled down.

I decided to wait until the next morning to contact Hacker about Rico's deal. I had no doubts Hacker would pay. On the other hand, I wasn't sure whether I wanted to be the conduit for what might be blood money. There was always the option of taking Lila back to the States and then advising Hacker what I might do to him if I found out he was molesting her. For most guys, that would do the job. In Hacker's case, though, it would probably result in some flunky taping a pipe bomb to the undercarriage of my new Roadmaster. Trying to lean on Hacker would have all the effect of hitting a bonfire with a seltzer bottle full of kerosene.

I stripped off my shoulder rig, peeled out of my sweat-sodden clothes, and took a cool shower. After toweling off, I pulled open the underwear drawer of the dresser, looking for a new pair of skivvies.

Immediately, I realized something was wrong.

I rifled the drawer quickly. Hemingway's revolver was missing. I had stashed it in the drawer after Marisol asked me to put it away the evening before. Jaime had returned my Colt so I didn't really need it.

There were only two options. Either someone had tossed my room and found the gun — which I doubted, since I'm pretty good at noticing when a room's been ransacked, even by experts — or the gun had been taken by the only person who had been in the room since I'd left to meet Rico.

Marisol.

Chapter Eighteen

I could only guess what Marisol might want with the revolver. As close as Hector was to Batista, acquiring weapons would be easy for him. He'd also need plenty of firepower on his sugar plantations, to ward off gleaners and poachers and to dispatch vermin, if for no other reason. If she needed a gun, she could find one about anywhere on her estates.

Unless, of course, she needed one that couldn't be traced.

Did she want it for protection? What if she planned to tell Hector that they were through, and she was going back to Florida with me? The way Hector felt about me, he was capable of doing practically anything in retaliation. Maybe she wanted to be sure she could stop him if he decided to try to force her to stay.

Chances were I was giving myself way too much credit. If there was anything or anyone

Marisol loved more than me, it was Cuba itself. She had the inside track to the highest offices on the island. Batista had turned paradise into a brothel. It was because of Batista's repression of his own people that Castro and his cronies were hacking and burning their way through the jungles toward Havana. What if Marisol believed that, by doing away with Batista, she might save her homeland from the reds? Was she willing to take on the role of assassin and martyr to save her beloved island?

There were way too many variables. The one thing certain was that the gun Hemingway had given me was now in Marisol's hands. I couldn't see any way for that to turn out well. I needed to find her as quickly as possible.

I could have tried to reach her through Rico, but what would I tell him? *By the way, Rico, after I slept with your sister-in-law last night she stole my gun?*

What had Rico said the other night, after taking a *pelota* to the head? He had said that he lived with Hector and Marisol in the Miramar District, perhaps only a few blocks from the Hilton. It was possible I could look out my window and see their villa. He'd also said that Hector spent all his time at the Presidential Palace.

I decided to call Jaime Guzman, reasonably certain that anything I told him would stay between us.

When the switchboard operator at police headquarters connected me with him, he said, "I do hope you are calling to tell me you have completed your job, and are headed home."

"Not yet, but soon, I hope. I need to know where Rico Gonzalez lives."

"You, of course, are referring to Rico Gonzalez who is the brother of Hector Gonzalez, are you not?"

"That's the one."

"The man who is also the brother-in-law of Marisol Gonzalez?"

"I don't have time to play games, Jaime. Rico has a line on Cecil Hacker's daughter and he wants to make a deal. I need to know where to find him."

"Have you considered checking the Fronton Jai Alai?"

"He's off the card for a couple of weeks. Got hit in the head with a *pelota.* We met for breakfast this morning and he left without giving me his address. Do you know where he lives or not?"

I had inadvertently triggered that suspicious synapse in Jaime's detective brain.

"You sound desperate, my friend," he said.

"Are you in trouble? Do you need my assistance — beyond giving you Rico's address, that is?"

"I have things under control," I lied.

"If that is the case, then you may be a singular case in this city. Against my better judgment, I'll tell you that Rico, along with his brother and sister-in-law, lives at one-four-seven-two Lagunas in Centro Habana, the Miramar District. I know this because I have been a guest at his home on several occasions. Perhaps I could escort you there — as a courtesy, of course."

"No need. I'll probably give him a phone call. I needed an address for the operator."

"I see," Jaime said, with a hesitance in his voice that suggested his suspicion that I had lied to him.

"Don't worry," I said. "I want to wrap up this case and get stateside before . . ."

I stopped as I realized I was talking to a cop on a police-station telephone in a country known for its corruption. Jaime could have been as coy as I had been. In any case, I sure didn't want to leave any eavesdroppers with the impression that both Jaime and I expected regime change in the near future.

"Before Christmas, of course." Jaime finished the sentence for me.

"Yes. Christmas. It would be nice to be home for the holidays."

"No doubt. Please feel free to contact me again should you need any assistance."

"Thanks," I said, and rang off.

Now I had another decision to make. I could place a call to the Gonzalez residence and hope that Hector didn't answer the phone. However, if I reached Marisol, what would I say to her? "Did you steal my gun and, if you did, who do you plan to shoot?"

It didn't seem like a good conversation starter.

The other option was to go to her home, scout the place out first to make sure Hector wasn't around, and then confront Marisol. If she had the gun, I'd take it from her. I'd already resolved that it didn't matter *why* she had taken it. It wasn't hers and it wasn't mine, and I would be damned if I was going to let her do something violent with it.

I wound up taking a cab over to Lagunas. I'd have been a lot happier with wheels of my own. It's easier to do a stakeout from a car. A guy — especially an American — loitering on the street outside somebody's house in Havana looks pretty damned suspicious after a while.

I was lucky. The Gonzalez compound — and that's what it was, a main house with a collection of smaller *cabanas* and outbuildings surrounding it — was situated across from a public park. I have great eyesight, so I strolled into the park and found a bench that gave me a reasonable view of the house.

The day was overcast, which was fine by me. It was Christmas Eve, which in most of the United States meant overcoat weather, but in the tropics the sun could bake you in the deep midwinter. Besides, the clouds gave me a bit of cover. I wasn't uncomfortable, which meant I could keep my lookout for an extended time.

I needn't have worried. I'd only been scouting the house for about a quarter hour when a car pulled up the drive and into the circular turnaround near the front door. A uniformed chauffeur stepped out and walked up to the shaded porch, where he rang the doorbell. Moments later, Hector Gonzalez stepped out of the house and down to the car, followed closely by the chauffeur, who held the back door for him as Hector slid into the seat.

It had been six years since I had cleaned his clock. High living and good food had put some weight on him. Even from a distance, I could see the graying at his temples, and the heaviness of his steps. He hadn't been much of an opponent during my last visit to Havana, so I wondered why the sight of him made me so apprehensive.

Probably the fact that I had slept with his wife, and that he now wielded a hell of a lot more clout.

As the car pulled onto the street, I could see the official government markings on the rear as well as the black-and-white government plates. It looked like Hector had business with Batista. Things being what they were, a good guess was that he'd be occupied for some time.

I folded the *La Priensa* newspaper I had thoughtfully brought with me and ambled out of the park, trying to appear leisurely even as I made a beeline toward the Gonzalez home.

A smart man might have been more cautious, taken some time to reconnoiter the property, make sure there weren't armed guards or lookouts lying in wait for uninvited intruders. In retrospect, a smart man wouldn't have allowed himself to be deprived of Hemingway's revolver in the first place, so this — obviously — wasn't a smart man's endeavor.

I crossed Lagunas, walked up to the front porch, and rang the doorbell, exactly as I had seen the chauffeur do moments earlier.

It seemed like hours before the door opened. During that time, I felt horribly exposed. After all, anyone — especially anyone connected with Hector — could see me.

A woman in a gray, short-sleeved dress and an apron answered the door. I asked, in my neglected Spanish, to see her mistress. She stepped aside and gestured for me to step inside, and then she hustled toward the rear of the house.

The interior of the house was dusky, with drapes drawn to ward off the heat of the day, and it smelled old. Not dirty or decayed, just old, the way that homes of the wealthy often do. In multigenerational homes, furniture tends to be passed down from one era to the next, and the Gonzalez family had been strong and influential for well over a century.

I heard a gasp at the end of the hallway, and I turned to see Marisol. She wore a striped blouse with sleeves that ended below her elbows, and a brown skirt that hugged her hips like a frightened child. Her legs were bare and cinnamon colored, and they glistened as if they had been oiled. Her hair was pulled back in a ponytail.

She looked at the servant who had ushered

me into the house. "It's all right," she said. "I know the gentleman. He and my husband are acquainted."

The maid returned to her duties. For a moment Marisol stared at me. Then she crossed the expanse of carpeted hallway that bisected the house, her hands stiffly at her side.

"Please, Mr. Smith, step into the parlor," she said, as she gestured to the room on her right. Obviously, she didn't want the help to hear my real name. Why? Because the allegiances under the Gonzalez roof were not dependable?

I led her into the room and she pulled the French doors closed behind her.

"What are you doing here, Mac? Hector left a few minutes ago. If he had seen you —"

"I waited for him to leave. I was sitting on a bench in the park, watching the house. I'm not stupid."

"Coming here at any time is the definition of stupidity! In Havana, you have a distinctive look. If the woman who let you in describes you to Hector, he will know who you are immediately. What were you thinking?"

"Where is it?" I asked, ignoring her question.

“Where is what?”

“The revolver that was in the drawer in my hotel room. I placed it there last night, when you told me to put it away. After I met with Rico this morning, I went back to the hotel and it was gone. You were alone in the room after I left. What are you planning to do with the gun, Marisol?”

“I have no idea what you are talking about. I did exactly as you said. I waited a half hour after you left and then I came home. I know nothing about any gun.”

I reached out, grabbed her by the arms, and drew her to me. Any other time I’d have been overwhelmed by the scent of her, but this time I was furious.

“You don’t understand! The gun doesn’t belong to me. It belongs to a very important man. You are the only person who could have taken it, and I’m going to get it back, even if I have to take this house apart brick by brick. Do you hear me? I don’t know what kind of harebrained scheme you’ve hatched, but I’m not going to be a part of it. Now where is it?”

“I want you to leave,” she said. “Now I see that coming to you last night was a mistake. To think I was planning to go with you back to Florida. And now, you accuse me of . . . what? Plotting murder? What on earth would I want with your gun?"

"How in hell would I know? Maybe you wanted to kill Hector. Maybe you planned to martyr yourself and take out Batista. Maybe you wanted a quick way out in case the reds storm Havana and it looks like they might take you captive. All I know is that I can't be part of it. All I want is the revolver. We'll work everything else out another time. Now, will you go get it or do I need to toss the entire house?"

"That won't be necessary," someone said from the doorway.

I knew who he was even before I turned.

Rico stood at the door. His eyes were shiny from too many daiquiris, too soon in the afternoon. He grinned malevolently as he surveyed me with Marisol. Then he reached up and scratched at his cheek with the barrel of Hemingway's revolver.

CHAPTER NINETEEN

I had my Colt automatic drawn and cocked almost before I was aware of what I was doing. Years of experience and training took over. I wasn't about to stand there and allow Rico to have any advantage over me.

"Hand it over," I said. "It doesn't belong to you."

He ignored me, ignored my gun, merely said, "Have you spoken with your client in Miami about my offer? Is he willing to pay to have his daughter returned to him?"

"I was sidetracked," I said, which was only a small lie. "I got back to the hotel and found someone had looted my room. I thought it was Marisol. Give me the gun, Rico. Now!"

"You won't shoot me. I'm your conduit to the girl. Tell you what. We shall be gentlemen. You put away your pistol and I will set this ugly piece of iron on the table, and we shall have a nice talk, eh?"

I didn't holster my weapon. I did, however, raise the barrel toward the ceiling. Rico seemed confused for a few seconds, and then he grinned again. "I see. We shall learn to trust one another in little steps. See? I can be reasonable."

He placed the revolver on the table next to him.

"You stole the gun, Rico?"

"Not personally. I was with you, remember? First at La Bodeguita del Medio and then at the church. Well, of course I was not *with* you at the church. But I know you were there. I trust you had an enlightening conversation with Señor McCarl? He tells an interesting story, doesn't he?"

"How did you get the gun?"

"I have friends. Some of them work at the Hilton hotel. Before I called you this morning, I asked one of my *friends* to take a look at your room after you left. I thought, perhaps, she might discover some information I'd find useful. She brought me the gun. Why she decided to take it, I haven't a clue. She did tell me an interesting story, however. It seems, as she entered the hallway to go to your room, your door opened. She was nervous, so she slipped into an empty room using her master key. Imagine her surprise when she saw who walked out of your room and hurried to the stairway."

Marisol turned away from both of us. She braced herself against a column as her hand covered her mouth. Her eyes betrayed her terror.

"My sister-in-law is well-known," Rico continued. "My friend recognized her immediately. And now, it appears, I have provided you with some more motivation to get Mr. Hacker to meet my demands, no? After all, if I am in Florida, and if I have enough money to allow me to live my life by my terms, what reason would I have to betray Marisol to her husband?"

"Give him whatever he wants," Marisol pleaded, though she still couldn't look at me. "He is ruthless and lazy. He'd tell Hector about us if it were to his advantage."

"I was right to tell McCarl not to trust you," I said to Rico. "You're a snake."

"Mac! Is that any way to talk to a friend? Please believe me, your secret is safe with me. I love you like a brother. And — whether you believe it or not — I do think Marisol would be much happier with you than with Hector. Perhaps I can help make that happen for you. First, though, you have to help *me*. A sign of good faith —" He gestured toward the revolver, and then stepped away from the table.

I scooped up the revolver and slipped it into my jacket pocket.

"Here's the way it's going to be," I told Rico. "I'll approach Hacker. I'll tell him your offer. If he accepts, you won't get a penny until you produce the girl. All I've seen so far is McCarl. He seems devoted to Lila, but for all I know it's an act and he's already tossed in with you. Whatever. I'll talk with Hacker, but I need to see Lila or the deal dies."

Rico held both hands up, palms out. "What more could I ask from a friend?"

"There's more. You forget what your housemaid girlfriend saw at the Hilton. You talk with her and make sure *she* forgets it, too. That's not part of this. Hacker might meet your demands and he might not. I'm betting he will. The money doesn't mean anything to him and he wants his daughter back. If I ever find out you told Hector or anyone else about Marisol being in my room, I'll find you and kill you. You hear me? I've killed people in Cuba before, Rico. The way things are right now, in a few days there are likely to be a lot of bodies lying around. One more random killing won't even be noticed. You shoot off your mouth and I'll shoot off your head. Is there anything in that you don't understand?"

A cloud seemed to pass over his face and then he waggled a finger at me. "Call Mr. Hacker, Mac. Until we have a deal, it would be crazy for me to — how do you say? — double-cross you. I can't collect my finder's fee if I am dead! You'd better be quick. I have a tendency toward impatience. I'll leave you and my sister-in-law alone now."

He stepped out of the parlor and closed the doors.

Marisol had taken a seat in an overstuffed wing chair near the drawn window.

"I am finished," she said, her voice breaking. "Hector will murder me."

"Not if he can't get to you. I meant what I said. You have to come back to Florida with me. There isn't any other way now. You know Rico can't be trusted. Sooner or later, he'll get too drunk to hold his tongue, or you'll make him angry and he'll roll over on you just to cross you. Besides, if Hector stays in Cuba he's going to die, and soon. One way or the other, you're free to come away with me. I'll make the deal with Hacker. We'll send his daughter back to him, if that's what it takes to get you away from this island."

Bent over at the waist, her arms wrapped around her stomach, she stared at the floor and shook her head back and forth. For a moment I thought she might be sick.

"Leave," she said.

"Tell me you'll come to Florida."

"Leave me!" she wailed. "This is as much my fault as it is yours. I never should have come to your room. Now I'm ruined."

I knelt in front of her and tried to catch her eye. She refused to look at me.

"You aren't ruined. This is your way out. You can leave tonight. I'll give you the keys to my place in Miami. You can fly out on the first plane and wait for me to finish what I have to do here. It won't take more than a few days. Havana is going to burn, Marisol. You won't recognize it a year from now. Batista can't stop it. Nobody can. If you wait too long, you'll miss your chance."

"I . . . cannot . . . think," she said. "Go away. Let me think. Nothing makes any sense anymore."

I stood but I couldn't will my legs to walk. "I'm going back to the hotel," I said. "I'm going to contact my client and I'm going to get Rico his money. As soon as I have the girl, I'll be coming for you. I want you to be ready to leave. It could come any time. Understand?"

She shook her head. "I don't know what to do. Please leave. Give me time to think."

There was no use arguing or cajoling. I

wasn't going to sway her with words. She needed time to come to her senses and realize she only had one reasonable choice.

And I had things to do.

I let myself out of her house.

Chapter Twenty

The streets of the Miramar District were mostly empty. It was Christmas Eve, and families were gathered in their homes, their holiday celebrations perhaps tempered by apprehensions about the future. They had good reason to worry.

I was forced to hoof it back to the Hilton. It wasn't far, but it gave me a lot of time to think.

This whole job was quickly degenerating into a quagmire of bad decisions — starting, I realized, with my own agreement to take Cecil Hacker's case. Coming to Havana had always been a bad idea.

I'm a private cop. Most of the time I take money from people to confirm their worst fears and suspicions. A child runs away from home, falls in with people whose values seem to flow backwards from a sewer, and sometimes it falls on my shoulders to tell the parents their hopes and dreams for the future have been consumed by a world they never imagined existed. Someone suspects the man or woman they married and vowed to stand by through sickness and health has been knocking off a little side action with a boss or a secretary or — worse — a trusted friend. I take their money and provide them with facts and photos that make them believe their hearts have been ripped from their chests with a garden rake.

I make my living off of the desperation of others. I don't typically worry much about it, or even give it much thought. Most people don't have the stuff it takes to do the tough work, the things that have to be done. They aren't strong enough, or big enough, or maybe even smart enough to know how to navigate the world of shadowed alleys and darkened doorways, to negotiate the environs of people whose souls are blacker than volcanic obsidian.

It takes a while, but with time you burn out the nerve endings that respond to the distress of others. Sympathy gives way to cynicism. Trust becomes something other people do, and which you know will someday betray them. True love becomes a farce indulged in by the deluded and the naïve, founded on rationalization and self-serving infatuation, and doomed to disaster.

I usually don't give a damn. I take the money, I do the job, and I walk away and leave my clients to pick up the pieces of their lives. Caring too much costs you that precious half second that can spell the difference between waking the next morning and the permanent silence of the grave.

Everything else I leave to social workers and psychiatrists and others who are paid to care.

What McCarl had told me was a new one. This business with Lila Hacker bothered me. On the one hand, it was a job, not a lot different than any other I'd taken over the years. I was no stranger to con artists, hucksters, sneak thieves, mobsters, blackmailers, bootleggers, sex fiends of every stripe, even murderers. Sure, I had run up against child molesters, pederasts and incestuous parents. You see all types in this business. None of them had ever hired me, and no one had ever hired me to bring a victim back from the lam.

I had hired Nelson Aquilino, back in Miami, to check out Cecil Hacker because I knew I wasn't inclined to return a fourteen-year-old kid to the world of hurt and degradation that Danny McCarl had implied would come to her at the hands of her father. A sucker might have fallen for his story outright, but I wanted it verified.

And yet, here I was, hogging my way back to the Hilton with every intention of selling Hacker on a plan to pay off Rico. Why? Because it was my job? Or because sacrificing Lila Hacker's innocence was the only way I could get Marisol off of Cuban soil and permanently in my arms in Miami?

The farther I got from Miramar and the hypnotic effect Marisol had on me, the worse I liked myself.

In a perfect world, I'd get back to the hotel and find a note from Aquilino telling me that — at least sexually — Hacker was clean as a whistle.

I'd given up on perfect worlds in the mud of Anzio. I needed an alternate plan.

Chapter Twenty-One

There were no messages for me at the Hilton's front desk. I suppose I wasn't surprised. I'd only put Aquilino on the case a few hours earlier. He's good, but he's not Superman. It would take time for him to run down the hot poop and straight skinny on Hacker, especially on Christmas Eve.

The sun had started to set during my walk back. Every ballroom in the hotel was swinging with live bands and dinner parties. The parties had spilled out into the hotel lobby. I hadn't eaten since my breakfast with Rico, but there were lines outside the two hotel restaurants. I'm not much for standing in lines, not since I got out of the Army in '46.

I was thinking of ordering a sandwich at the bar when a bellhop carrying a telephone passed through the crowd.

"Mr. Loame!" he shouted. "Telephone call for Mr. Loame!"

What in hell?

I waved him down and he directed me to an alcove off the main lobby, where he plugged the telephone into a jack and accessed the switchboard. Then he handed me the receiver.

I slipped him a peso for his trouble and then spoke into the phone.

The voice on the other end said, "This is Hacker. I've been trying to reach you all day."

"If you'd been able to find me, it would mean I wasn't doing my job. I don't lounge around the hotel lobby waiting for leads to drop in my lap."

"Of course. Do you have any news?"

Fate had robbed me of my time for deliberation. I knew things I wasn't certain I wanted to share with him. On the other hand, he was the client.

"There's a lead. There's a guy down here who may know where your daughter is, but he wants a deal."

"What kind of deal? What's his name?"

I decided a couple of lies mixed in with the truth would keep me an inch or two on the dingy side of grace.

"He wants to remain anonymous for the moment. He's well connected, from a prominent family, and he doesn't want word to get back to them. Like everyone else on the island he's looking for a way out. He's thinking of coming to Florida and needs a stake to get started."

"How big a stake?"

"A hundred grand."

"That's a lot," said Hacker after a short pause.

"It's up to you. I'm passing along what I've learned. It's your money and your daughter. This guy is used to the good life. He isn't going to be satisfied with living in some bungalow on the outskirts of the Everglades."

"You think his information is good?"

"If you're asking whether I trust him, Mr. Hacker, the answer is no, though in this case I think he's telling the truth. He showed me a picture of your daughter, with proof it was taken yesterday. Here's the way the deal would work. You agree to give him the money and set up a bank account in Miami. Soon as he gets a cable from the bank that the money is deposited, he'll take me to Lila and I can bring her home."

"What if he cheats me? What if I make the deposit and he disappears?"

"It's my job to make sure that doesn't happen. I'm your man on the ground here in Havana. You pay this guy off and he doesn't produce, I'll see to it he never sees a penny of the money."

Another pause.

"I knew I was right about you," Hacker finally said. "You *are* the kind of tough guy I needed for this job. You're my kind of man."

I suppressed a wave of nausea and the push of hot wash in my gullet.

"Luck of the draw, Mr. Hacker. You want some time to think this over?"

Part of me wanted him to think about it, very carefully. I still needed a cushion of time to work through all of my options and I hadn't expected to deal with Hacker so quickly. Also, if he hesitated it would tell me a lot about how much he really wanted Lila back.

"You find this guy," Hacker said. "You tell him he has a deal. You tell him I'll pay his price."

"There's another problem," I said.

"What's that?"

"It's after five o'clock on Christmas Eve. The banks are closed tomorrow and Friday for the holidays. You can't make the deposit until Monday. That's the soonest I can work things out with my guy."

"Damn! I forgot about the holiday."

"I have an idea, if you're open to it."

"Will it get Lila back to me?"

"It's a risk. I can't do the deal until Monday at the earliest. That doesn't mean I have to sit around here, twiddling my thumbs and drinking on your nickel. I can do some surveillance on my guy. He might lead me to Lila without you having to shell out."

"What's the risk?"

"If I get made, he could rabbit on me. Or, he might contact McCarl and tell him to get out of town. We might lose our best link to your daughter."

"Then you don't get made. Understand? I'm depending on you here."

His meaning was clear. If I blew the play, he'd take it out of my hide. I didn't care. I'd bought myself the time I needed to figure out what I was going to do.

"I'll be careful. I'm a professional, Mr. Hacker. I do this for a living. I don't get made often."

"See that you don't. Call me when you have the information on the bank account. I'll do whatever it takes to get Lila home."

He didn't bother saying good-bye. He cut the line and I was left holding a dead receiver.

I dropped it into the cradle, and stared at it. Did I intend to shadow Rico for the next couple of days? Or was I trying to convince Hacker I wasn't dragging my butt around down in the tropics?

At some level, I wanted to find Lila whether I was going to take her back to Miami or not. I don't like leaving jobs unfinished. Beyond that, all I had to go on was some story told me by McCarl, who had spirited her out of the country in the first place. I'd heard lots of sob stories from plenty of guilty guys over the years. Some of them had been pretty convincing. Few of them had been true. I wanted to hear Lila tell me her story. At age fourteen, she was probably unpracticed at artifice and I'd have an easier time determining whether or not she was being truthful.

Also, now I had time for Nelson Aquilino to pull together some more information on Hacker.

I felt more relieved than I had when I had returned to the hotel.

My relief didn't last very long. I turned to head back into the lobby and found my path blocked by Hector Gonzalez.

Chapter Twenty-Two

One thing was certain. I wasn't going to let him intimidate me.

"Hector," I said. I nonchalantly placed my hands on my hips, which also served to open my jacket enough to display my shoulder rig and the .38 automatic.

"I heard the bellboy call your name. A name like that, there can be only one man, eh?"

"Something I can do for you?" I asked, as I worked my way past him into the lobby.

He fell into step beside me, not in a collegial way, but rather to keep me within striking distance.

"What are you doing in Havana?" he asked.

"I'm working." I pulled a copy of Lila's picture from my jacket pocket. "I don't suppose you've seen this girl."

He scarcely glanced at the picture.

"I am here with the minister of commerce," he said. "We're entertaining a group of Argentine investors."

"You're busy, then. Don't let me keep you."

I started to walk away, but he placed a hand on my shoulder. It was the wrong thing to do. I grabbed it and turned quickly, twisting it into what could be an excruciating angle — a little trick I'd learned during hand-to-hand combat training at Parris Island. At the same time, I slipped my right hand under my jacket to the butt of the .38.

"Do you really want to start trouble here, Hector?"

His eyes narrowed but he refused to betray fear, or even discomfort. "I am bored with the meeting," he said. "I was about to invite you to dinner."

I searched his face for any sign of mockery. I also scanned the room for any security forces who might have been alerted by my borderline assault on one of Batista's most trusted. I didn't see either.

I released his hand.

"I could eat," I told him.

There were two restaurants in the hotel. Hector led me past the line at Trader Vic's and across the lobby to a high-class supper club. There was a line there too, but as soon as Hector presented himself to the host at the front desk, there was a sudden scurry and we were seated.

"I get this kind of service in Miami," I said as a waiter filled our water glasses.

"No doubt. How long has it been? Six years?"

"More or less. I haven't been counting. Are we eating on Batista's tab?"

"We're eating on *my* tab."

"In that case, what's good here?"

"It's a Hilton. They hire only the finest chefs. Everything is good."

I glanced over the menu. It took me about thirty seconds to choose the Delmonico steak.

"So," I said. "How's tricks?"

"I cannot complain." Hector set down his menu. "Life has been good to me. Did you know I married Marisol?"

"Did you? How's that working out for you?"

I thought I saw a bit of a flush at the tips of his ears and I wondered how much he knew. Then he shook his head and took a sip of his water.

"Have you ever wanted something so badly that it never occurred to you what you would do with it if you acquired it?" he asked.

"Yes."

"Then you may understand. I am certain you know about Cuba's problems with internal stability. After President Batista took office —"

"You mean, after he booted Socorros."

"It is impolite to be rude to a man who is buying you dinner. I am sure you will agree that Havana — in fact, all of Cuba — has flourished under Batista."

"It's apparent some people have made a killing."

A wave of confusion crossed his features for a moment, and then he smiled. "Ah, yes. An American idiom. 'A killing.' Meaning some people have been enriched by the Batista administration."

"Sure. That's exactly what I meant."

"And you are correct. I am one of those people, in fact. My family, of course, has always had some prominence because of our sugar business. Under Batista, however, I have also acquired some political prestige."

"What does this have to do with Marisol?"

"It is . . . difficult for a man to serve two masters. In the same way, I have found there are complications associated with dividing my attentions between my civic responsibilities and my familial ones."

"But Marisol is understanding, I'm sure."

"How can one tell? I do fear that I have not been as attentive a husband as I might have been otherwise, or as she might desire."

"Priorities," I said. "It's a tough deal."

"I also should make it clear that — no matter how my attentions might be distracted by my duties to the government — I consider my marriage to Marisol to have been one of my most important achievements."

"You romantic devil."

"No. I know I am not romantic. Romance has never served me well. I am too grounded, too realistic to dwell on the games of love. I cannot see myself as a fawning, infatuated adolescent, and indeed I think I never was such a person. There is nothing I prize higher than my lovely wife and I do believe I could easily kill anyone who threatened to take her from me."

I leaned back in my seat and met Hector eye-to-eye. "We've been here before," I said. "As I remember, I showed you rather conclusively how intimidated I am by you. I'm sure you were devastated when Marisol returned to Miami with me."

Another wave of confusion, and then a flash of realization.

"I see. You are being sarcastic. Yes, you won the fight, but I took the prize."

"That's right. And it was six years ago. The world has changed a lot since then."

"In many ways. Are you sure that girl" — he gestured toward my breast pocket, where I kept Lila Hacker's pictures — "is the only reason you are in Havana?"

"A week ago I planned to spend the holidays on the beach in Miami in the company of a bottle of Jose Cuervo and a bowl full of limes. If it weren't for this job, and if the money I'm being paid to do it weren't so good, I'd be there. I've had six years to come back to Havana if I wanted to. And while we're on the subject, if I had wanted to steal your wife from you, I'd have done it long before now. The fact is, I didn't even know when I came to Cuba that you and Marisol had married. I haven't heard from her since nineteen fifty-two."

"A pity."

"For whom? Look, Hector, I'm hungry and I'm already tired of Havana, and I would like to go home before Castro and his pals occupy Batista's bedroom. The last thing I want to do is get in a pissing match with you, especially since you're picking up the bill for dinner. I only want to find the girl, and take her back to her father."

"Fair enough. We shall not speak of Marisol again. I believe, as distasteful as I find you, that you are a man of your word. Besides, it would be a shame to waste such a fine meal on rivalry and recriminations."

"I think you've made your position clear."

"One more thing. Don't be so certain our political circumstances in Cuba are as bleak as you portray them. We have dealt with insurrections before. Now, have you considered which wine we should order?"

All things considered, it was probably the strangest meal I'd ever had. After his initial posturing and chest puffery, and after he apparently was satisfied he had made his suspicions toward me known, Hector became almost cordial and, after a couple of glasses of wine, even eerily gregarious.

For my part, I sipped at my wine and kept the path to my automatic clear. Men like Hector were never willing to let old scores go unsettled, and I had left him humiliated six years earlier.

However, when our dinner was over he paid the check, swallowed the last of the wine, and swiped at his mouth with the napkin.

"I would like to say this has been pleasant," he said. "Of course, it has not. Despite that, I am a civilized man and I am not necessarily the same man I was at our last meeting. I had no idea you were in Cuba. When I heard the bellboy call your name, I decided I should put our differences to rest. I do trust that, over dinner, we have both made our positions clear."

"I don't think you've left anything to question."

"And, more than anything else, at this time of crisis for my country, I did not wish you to be a distraction. I hope you enjoy good fortune in locating your runaway girl, because then you will return quickly to the United States, where I do not have to be concerned with you."

"Thanks."

"Yes. If you will excuse me, I must return to the minister of commerce and our Argentine guests. The duties of state, you understand."

He rose and turned to leave. As he wended his way through the supper club toward the lobby, I made a gun with my hand and pantomimed shooting him a couple of times in the back.

"Yeah," I said, to his retreating figure. "I understand you fine, you son of a bitch. But I'm still going to steal your wife."

Chapter Twenty-Three

By the time I left the supper club it was almost nine o'clock. I checked the front desk to see if Nelson Aquilino had left me a message. Still nothing.

I knew Hector was occupied in one of the meeting rooms with his Argentine cronies, and probably would be for at least a couple of hours. I grabbed a taxi at the stand outside the hotel and directed the driver to take me over to Lagunas.

When we arrived, I told the hack driver to wait for me and walked rapidly up to the front door of the main house at the Gonzalez compound. Rico opened the door on the second ring.

"Mac! Welcome to our home on this lovely Christmas Eve!"

I could smell the rum on his breath from two feet away.

"Walk with me," I told him.

He pulled the door shut and followed me

off the front gallery and down the steps. I held a finger up to the cabbie, telling him to wait a few more minutes. Then I led Rico into the park across the street. Even at night, I had no idea what eyes might be watching the front of Hector's house.

"Marisol and I are planning to attend the Christmas midnight mass at our church in a couple of hours," Rico said. "Perhaps you would like to join us."

"Fat chance," I said. "You're going to church smelling like a distillery?"

"I have not had so much to drink. So, do you have news for me?"

"The girl's father is going for the deal, but there's a snag. Tomorrow is Christmas. The banks are closed for the holidays until Monday. That's four days. He can't make a deposit until then."

"I am patient."

"I'm not. I want to wrap this matter up as soon as possible. I can't put ninety miles of water between me and Cuba soon enough. I want to go ahead and set up the arrangements."

"What arrangements?"

"How we're going to do the deal. Once you get confirmation the money has been deposited in your Florida account, how do you get the girl to me?"

He stroked his chin for a moment. "We'll work it out between now and then."

"And what about McCarl? Somehow, I can't imagine he'd just let her go."

"Mr. McCarl won't be an issue. I have friends who will see to it he does not interfere with our plans."

"You can guarantee that?"

"Does it matter? You don't intend to let him keep you from returning the girl, do you? If I don't get him out of the way, you will."

I paced back and forth and then realized something. "You haven't answered a single question directly, Rico. I have to wonder whether you still have the girl under your control."

"I do."

"You'd better be right. I want to make something clear to you. If Hacker pays your end and you don't deliver, the reds will be the least of your worries. Your hundred grand is probably mob money, which means you're obligated to produce. If you don't get me the girl, some of Hacker's employees are going to start looking for you. You cross me and I won't lift a finger to help you."

He grinned, and patted me on the cheek a couple of times. He was lucky not to draw back a stump.

"Don't worry, Mac. Everything is under control. Are you certain you don't want to come to mass?"

I gave him my most intimidating scowl and — without another word — turned around and walked up the hill to the cab.

"Take me back to the Hilton," I told the cabbie.

We were halfway to the hotel when I became aware of the weight of Hemingway's revolver in my coat pocket.

"Wait," I said. "I need to make a side trip."

I told him to take me to San Francisco de Paula, and directed him to *Finca Vigia,* Hemingway's estate.

From the road I could see lights on in the house and there were shadows of figures moving about. I hoped I wasn't about to crash a party of some sort.

I paid the driver and asked him to wait a few minutes, then made my way up the stone-and-shell path to the front patio.

The door opened seconds after I rang the bell. A blonde woman who came roughly to my chin smiled at me.

"Good evening! We're so glad you were able to make it! Please come in," she said.

I followed her inside, and removed my hat.

"I'm sorry," I said. "I wasn't exactly

invited. My name is Cormac Loame. I met Mr. Hemingway a few days ago, and I had to return something to him."

She held out her hand. "I'm Mary," she said. "Let's see if we can find my husband somewhere about."

As she led me into the main room where Hemingway and I had talked on my last visit, I saw ten or fifteen people talking and laughing. Hemingway stood behind a bar, pouring drinks. He looked up and met my eyes.

"Ah, at last, we have some life in the house! Loame, come on over and have a drink. I see you've met the missus."

I thanked Mary for bringing me in and walked over to the bar.

"I have something for you," I said, pulling the revolver from my pocket.

He shoved a highball glass into my hand.

"A trade, then!" he bellowed.

I sipped at the drink. It seemed to be mostly Bombay gin and ice, and from the flavor it appeared someone in the room had whispered the words *tonic water,* and a syllable or two had fallen into the glass.

"Got your gun back, then?" Hemingway asked.

"The police gave it to me yesterday. I meant to return your revolver before now, but it, well, disappeared briefly. I had to track it down."

"Someone stole my gun? This is a story I'd like to hear."

He led me to a corner, where I told him how a friend had spied on my hotel room, and how his agent had walked off with the revolver. I left out the part about my affair with Marisol.

"Then it's a good thing you brought it home," Hemingway said. "It wouldn't do to have strange firearms wandering about Havana at a time like this. Tell me, have you found that little girl you came for?"

"I think so. Look, I didn't want to crash your Christmas party. I have a taxi waiting outside —"

"Nonsense! You may be the most interesting person here. Now that we have you, we can't let you get away without meeting our guests. Mary!"

Mary, who had been talking with a short swarthy man on the other side of the room, turned and glared at her husband.

"Mr. Loame is staying for a while. Can we send someone out to tell his taxi to go?"

She nodded and walked over toward the door.

"Look at me," Hemingway said. "Stupid old man. There's no one to tell. No servants, you know. Don't worry, she'll send your cab packing. How's the drink?"

"It's fine."

"So, you got your gun back. Did they find out who plugged old Gopaldo?"

"Not yet."

"I'm glad it wasn't you, after all. Now, what about the girl?"

I told him I thought a deal was in place, but it would be Monday before it could be struck.

"That's a problem, Loame. You've been listening to the news?"

"Yes. The rebels —"

"Don't pay any attention to the news. They're all liars, in Batista's pocket. This revolution is going to happen, and it's going to be this week sometime." He held his own drink high and shouted, *"Viva la revolucion!"*

As if on cue, all the guests hoisted their own glasses and shouted, *"Viva la revolucion!"*

"Been doing that all goddamned evening," Hemingway told me, his voice slurred. "Most of the folk here tonight have one grudge or another against Batista. A relative put up against the wall at La Cabana here, another tortured wrongly there. After a while, a man like Batista makes a lot of enemies. Looks like any old Christmas party, doesn't it?"

"Isn't it?"

"It's a goddamned wake!" Hemingway roared. *"Viva la revolucion!"*

Almost like a litany, the crowd echoed the cry. For the first time, I noticed most of them weren't smiling.

"It's a farewell," Hemingway continued. "Most of the folks here are flying out of the country by the end of the weekend. Some for Florida, some for New York. Some are taking a boat over to the Caymans. They hate Batista and they're happy to see him go, but they're afraid of the rebels. They'll sit tight for a few months, gauge the mood in Cuba, and return if it seems all right. You're looking at the vanguard of Cuba's refugee movement. Hell, in a week or so you might run into one of these lovely folk in your local grocery store in Miami!"

"It's sad."

"It's supposed to be! It's a goddamned wake! Say, what are your plans? What are you going to do between now and Monday?"

"I'm hoping I can find the girl before my client has to pay a wad of money for her return. I don't trust the man who can take me to her."

"Well, you can't do any detecting tomorrow. Whole damned island is going to shut down for the holiday. Why don't you stay here? We can take the *Pilar* out for some *bonefishing* tomorrow. I know a place where the marlin fair near jump into the live well if you look at them the right way."

"It's tempting."

"Something to tell your goddamn grandchildren about, man! Christmas marlin fishing with Papa, on the eve of *la revolucion!*"

"La revolucion!" the party shouted.

It was the second strangest party I'd ever attended. My intent was to have a drink and make my polite apologies, then call a taxi and head back into the city. As I got closer to the bottom of my glass, the city seemed more and more like a silly place to spend Christmas alone, and by the end of the second drink I reached the conclusion that I owed myself a little break.

I passed out on the couch around three in the morning.

If I ever should have grandchildren, I will have to tell them about the Christmas Day I spent on the salt chasing the elusive marlin with Ernest Hemingway.

I woke that morning, still on the couch. Hemingway was slouched in a chair nearby, his hands crossed on his barrel chest. He seemed awake, but his eyes were focused somewhere in the distance.

"You alive?" I asked.

Slowly, he turned his head in my direction. "I should ask the same thing. Did I sleep here all night?"

"Hell, no. Most of the night you were drinking. You've only been there since the crack of dawn."

He slapped his thighs with his massive hands. "Then we must get going! Let's rustle up some breakfast and get to *Pilar* before the others decide they want to go too."

We didn't catch many fish, marlin or otherwise. This may have been because I spent a large portion of the first hour or so chumming the water with my breakfast. Hemingway had spent considerable time in Europe, and his idea of beginning a day following a night of drunken debauchery consisted mainly of kippers, eggs, brioche, butter and lots of coffee brewed to the pH of battery acid. Half a mile out from the marina, the azure waters of the Caribbean developed a wicked chop. I spent my fair share of time in the Army in WWII riding in rickety landing craft to several bullet-strewn beachheads, but never with a stomach full of herring packed in linseed oil.

After I had nothing left to disgorge, Hemingway pulled out a bottle of rum and a bag of limes. He also produced a foot and a half of French bread and tore off a hunk of one end.

"Nibble on that until you get your sea legs," he said. He didn't elaborate, probably because he didn't feel the need. He knew I was smart. He figured I didn't need additional coaching.

I sat in the marlin fishing seat near the stern transom. The seat was made of teak, curved to mold to the fisherman's back and bolted securely to the deck. In the front of the chair was a metal plate with a small swinging bucket, into which I would mount the rod, should we actually hook something large enough to fight back. There was a footrest mounted forward in the chair, and I had to straddle it. I leaned back and chewed slowly on small bites of the bread as Hemingway poured the rum into a jelly glass and squeezed in the juice from three or four limes. He steered the *Pilar* with one hand and drank with the other. I wondered how one man could drink so much without dying. It didn't seem to faze him, though, as he scanned the horizon, looking for any sign of flashing fins.

"I read one of your books," I said, after a few minutes.

"Do tell. I hear people do that from time to time. Which one?"

"A Farewell to Arms."

"Ah. That's the only one, then?"

"I read books, but there isn't a lot of time to make a constant habit of it."

"So, what did you think?"

"You want me to critique your book?"

"Why not? Seems to be growth business in that these days."

"I thought it was bleak."

"Bleak? That's all."

"It made me feel empty."

Hemingway glanced off to the starboard and steered the *Pilar* into the wind.

"I would have thought you might identify with Henry," he said.

"In what way?"

"He would have made a great private eye. Stoic, distant, fatalistic, nearly impenetrable. A man who drinks alone. A man who cannot see a future that contains himself in it."

I gnawed on the bread for a moment and reflected. "I didn't see him that way at all," I finally said. "Is that what you meant to write?"

"Hell, Loame, I don't know. It was thirty years ago. Sometimes I read words I wrote after the Great War, and they seem foreign to me. I marvel that I might have produced them. That bread helping your stomach?"

"Sure. I saw Henry as idealistic. I think he had beliefs, deep down. I think they kept him from being washed away in the tragedy of his life."

"That was the war. Trenches and foxholes were full of that kind of man. Most of them never came home. When did you read the book?"

"In high school in nineteen thirty-six."

"Before you went to war yourself."

"Yes."

"You saw action?"

"My share."

"Which theater?"

"Europe. Italy, Sicily. Did a tour in North Africa. Tunisia and Algeria."

"Dodged a few bullets in your time, then?"

"My share. Caught a few, too."

"Nobody gets lucky all the time. But I don't have to tell you that. You've been there. War makes heroes of the most ordinary people."

"I don't recall many heroes. Mostly, I remember a lot of guys terrified they'd never get home."

"What do you remember most?"

I took a swig of water from a wine bottle

next to me and pounded the cork back in with my palm. As I thought about his question, I lit a cigarette. The first drag burned my lungs and made my head spin, so I tossed it over the gunwale.

"What I remember most is something strange," I replied. "Not a battle, at least not one involving me. We were mopping up in Italy — this must have been nineteen forty-four. It had been tough, but we were advancing steadily. Rome was largely taken. But there were concerns about the monastery at Monte Cassino."

Hemingway cut the motors, and turned toward me. "You were at Monte Cassino?"

"I observed it. My unit wasn't directly involved. We were a couple of miles away, over a ridge, when the bombers appeared in the distance. It was like watching a swarm of locusts descending on the monastery. Then the bombs started to drop. They came in waves, line after line of incendiaries and HE, and then, between the aerial assaults, the artillery opened up. We watched for several hours as they took this amazing place that had stood there since the sixth century and turned it into a smoking heap of rubble and flames."

"Yes," Hemingway said. "They're skilled at that."

"But that wasn't it, the part I remember most. We all believed the monastery was swarming with Germans. The Allies bombarded it for two days. In the end, it turned out the only people in the monastery were a few monks and some villagers. A few of them survived, miraculously, and toward the end of the second day they finally got out. I saw them walking down the mountain, helping one another. Some of them were burned. Others had this look in their eyes I knew would never go away. There was an old man, looked about eighty, a monk, leading the way. The entire way down the mountain he prayed. Tell me something. After something like that, who do you pray to? Who do you praise, or thank, or beg for intervention, after your god allows that kind of thing to happen to you?"

"It's war," Hemingway said. "During wartime, you pray to the first god who will take your call."

"I remember reading *A Farewell to Arms,* back in high school. It made war sound like something honorable, in spite of the senselessness and the tragedy. I thought it glorified war."

"Glorified? Hardly."

"Then I went to war. You're right. There wasn't any glory there. In the end there were dead guys who had bought me drinks, and live guys who hadn't given me the time of day, and when it was over I came home to the realization that it was a matter of time before some idiot started it all over again."

"And, despite that, you took up a career of violence."

"There's not much violence to it. Well, sure, it happens from time to time, but most days I follow errant spouses or play peeping tom on guys trying to scam their insurance agencies on disability beefs. Once in a long while, usually when I think the case is simple, things get complicated and I have to resort to violence. It's not something I want to do. I don't go searching for it."

"Oh, horseshit!" he said, as he began to unpack the marlin gear from a storage bin on the midship gunwale. "Tell me you didn't come to Havana armed, and when your gun was taken from you the first thing you did was go and find a new one. And what about that business, sleeping with Gonzalez's wife? That's not inviting violence?"

I turned to him and stared. "How much did I drink last night?"

"Your share. You started talking about this Marisol woman on your third gin. Couldn't shut you up. What are you going to do about that?"

"Take her back to Miami."

"Going to drag her across the Florida Straits by her hair, are you?"

"If that's what it takes. It's what I should have done six years ago. It's time to set things straight."

He handed the heavy marlin rod to me and showed me the levers for releasing and locking the drag and the reel ratchet. He handed me a well-worn pair of leather gloves.

"Marlin strikes that line," he said, "and it'll spin off at a speed that will amaze you. Line running that fast is like a band saw. Slice your finger off in a second. The gloves will help you get home without losing your trigger finger, eh?"

We fed out the line, and Hemingway began a long, leisurely southern troll, running two or three knots, barely making time against the current, dragging the bait behind the boat.

"Ever seen a marlin on the line?" he asked, after a few minutes.

"No. I've caught some wahoo and bonita, and the occasional tuna."

"You're in for a treat, if we hook one today. Marlin's a smart, crafty fish. He might strike at the bait, and then again he might not. If he's hungry enough, you'll hook him fast and hard. Some fish follow the bait for a mile, sometimes more, sniffing it out. Once he decides to hit at it, his dorsal flares out like a geisha's fan and his wings spread and I swear to God you can see a smile on his face. He's a smart fish, all right. A mean fish, though. You don't toy with the blue . . ." He took another swig of rum, and returned to the wheel, five or six feet behind me.

We trolled for most of the day. For large parts of it, he stood at the wheel, gazing out at the sea as if he thought it might be his last glimpse ever. Other times, he would pull up a deck chair and talk about fishing, or hunting in Idaho.

We didn't talk about the war or about Marisol again.

Staying another night at *Finca Vigia* was probably a mistake. However, we had caught a few nice Spanish mackerel and one exceptional twenty-pound king that took me half an hour to land. Hemingway insisted I stay for dinner ("So we don't waste the catch," he argued), but I thought perhaps he wanted to talk more.

We gorged on grilled mackerel and Cuban

black beans with rice, tomatoes, and corn. Hemingway produced several bottles of Spanish *roja,* and by dinner's end we had uncorked all of them.

Toward the end of dinner, he turned on the shortwave and tuned it to Radio Rebelde. He listened intently as I tried to follow with my rusty Spanish. Slowly, his face turned dark.

"It's bad," he said. "They're attacking Santa Clara. That's the last barrier between Castro and Havana. It will all be over soon."

"Are you worried?" I asked.

"For myself? Hell, no. Six months from now, I'll probably take Castro out on the *Pilar.* We'll toss a few back, catch some fish. In all likelihood he'll sit right where you are now afterward. No, it's bad for Batista. Bad for my friends, the people you met last night. They dreamed of deposing Fulgencio for freedom, and look what a mess they're getting instead."

"How long?"

"Less than a week, I'd guess. Batista and his cronies are probably loading the pallets of booty on the planes as we speak. He can't pretend anymore. This day isn't his."

"I need to work fast, then. On Monday the banks open in Miami. As soon as my client transfers money to my contact in

Havana, I'm going to have to hustle the girl and Marisol off the island."

"I should drive you back to the city," Hemingway said. "But I'm not sure I can. Probably pass out on the way."

"Well, I'm in no shape to walk."

"Then it's settled. You stay here tonight and tomorrow we get you back to Havana so you can rescue your princess and spirit away your queen."

Chapter Twenty-Four

Hemingway dropped me off at the Hilton around nine the next morning. I showered, shaved, and changed into fresh clothes before calling the hotel operator to request a cable line to Miami. It was the day after Christmas and Nelson had been on the job for forty-eight hours. I needed an update, even though I had a feeling there wouldn't be much to report. Most of his contacts had probably been impossible to catch during the holiday.

It only took the operator a few minutes to clear a line. I asked the stateside operator to connect me with Nelson's number. He picked it up on the third ring.

"Where have you been?" he asked.

"You wouldn't believe it. Any word on Hacker?"

"Plenty. None of it good. He's in a shit-load of trouble, you know."

"I've heard the Feds might be looking at

his operation."

"Rumors say he's going to be indicted any day now."

"I'm not interested in his bookkeeping practices. I need to know whether it's safe to bring his daughter back to him."

"Probably not. Hacker must have a lot of juice here in South Florida. I had lots of doors slammed in my face. Started thinking it might not be safe to ask questions so openly. I did run down one lead, and it's troubling. A girl who works for one of the houses over on Calle Ocho told me she'd seen Hacker there several times. Said he has a yen for the young girls."

"How young?"

"Young enough to look too young, if you get my drift. There's some serious stuff bouncing around inside the Madman's head. I think there's a good chance he'd hit on his daughter if you brought her back."

"You're being objective here? This isn't you as a father talking?"

"I wouldn't allow Hacker within a city block of my girls, no. But the impression I got, talking to this girl over in Calle Ocho, is that he likes it rough. Sounds like Hacker isn't into the smooth, debonair approach. He's more likely to go after a girl with a whip and a chair. How is it you keep working for these lowlifes?"

I ignored him. "Stick with it," I said, "but be careful. You don't want to pull the wrong string and let the word get back to Hacker that you're poking around in his business."

"Trouble with the Madman is the last thing I need. I'll see what else I can find. You headed off the reservation again, or am I going to be able to find you?"

"I'll call you when I can. I have two more days to make a decision."

I rang off and walked out to the balcony to smoke a cigarette. It was Saturday morning, bright and sharp and clear. The sun angled off the transparent water of the Malecòn and reflected back in thousands of brilliant pinpoints. Somewhere in the city, Lila Hacker thought she was safe and protected. I had a feeling she might be in as much danger under Rico's wing as she might be if I returned her to Miami.

I've never been good with moral dilemmas. You spend enough years rooting through the muck and compost that constitutes the lives of people, and you begin to recognize that most folks' moral compasses possess no due north. We aren't so far descended from our arboreal ancestors that we've risen above avarice, greed, lust, and all the other flotsam of a savage heritage.

After a while, you start to see every lecherous glare in a bar, every lily-pale ring of skin on an otherwise deeply tanned finger, every sloe-eyed broad trolling for action as potential dollar signs and bank deposits. You know people are basically up to no good when they don't believe they're being observed, and it's a matter of time before their marriage or partnership or love life runs off the axle. That's when I come in. For the most part, I spy. I follow the philandering husband, the wayward wife, the embezzling employee, the fraudulent insurance-policy holder and the thieving heir. I take pictures and sometimes I take movies, and my office files overflow with the proof that people are among the least noble species of animals.

And what did that make me? An opportunist? An exploiter? Or something like a set of societal scales, trying to bring things back into balance. All I knew was that — more times than I liked to think — my decisions had been based more on economics than ethics. My moral boundaries could be as shifting as any others. I could see the world in ethically relative terms as easily as the next guy.

So why wasn't I following the money on this one? It was a simple case. Grab the girl.

Take her back to her father. Easy. Open and shut. I had done far worse in my career, and I could still look myself in the eye in my shaving mirror, at least most of the time.

Moral dilemmas give me headaches. I like my options clearly defined. At the moment, the choices I'd been dealt felt more like one of those Dali paintings with melting clock faces, or trying to play jacks with a quicksilver ball.

There was no point in debating it. I had a job to do and I would either do it or not. I couldn't make my decision at that moment because I still didn't know all the facts.

I stubbed the cigarette on the balcony rail, tossed it over and watched it fall to the ground ten floors below. Then I put on my jacket. I needed to get out in the world and clear all the brambles from my head. I needed some clarity.

Jaime Guzman and a burly uniformed cop intercepted me as I stepped off the elevator into the lobby.

"I need your gun again," he said. No greeting. No salutations. His face was grim, his skin gray, mottled by a day's growth of beard.

"Why?"

"This is one of those times when I will

suggest that you allow me to ask the questions. Where have you been for the past two days?"

"With friends. What's this about?"

"Your pistol, please."

By now the uniformed cop had his revolver out, against his thigh. Jaime's eyes told me volumes. Something bad had happened and there was pressure on him to fix it, quickly.

I pulled my gun out and handed it to him, butt first.

"Now," I said, "you want to tell me what's happened?"

"These friends of yours, they will vouch for you?"

"I'm pretty sure they will. For the moment I'd prefer to protect their privacy. If push comes to shove, we can bring them in. What do you think I've done?"

He stowed my pistol in his jacket pocket, then took me by the elbow and said, "You need to come with me. There has been trouble."

I had never seen Danny McCarl directly, except as a hazy shadow on the opposite side of the confessional, but I was pretty certain the body lying half covered by a pile of trash in the alley behind a *bodega* on the

Calle Los Empresas was him. The blond-tinted hair and the height looked right, and he was wearing the same summer-wool pants I had seen in the picture Rico had shown me.

"Yeah," I told Guzman. "I think it's him. What happened?"

"He was shot several times. This one did not require an elephant gun to bring him down."

Jaime was trying to make a joke of what I'd told him about Gopaldo, but at that moment I wasn't in a humorous mood.

"A thirty-eight-caliber?" I asked.

"We think. Not enough damage for a forty-five, and more than you'd expect with a twenty-five or a thirty-two. Now you know why I wanted your pistol."

"I haven't fired it. You can run a paraffin test on me if you want. I'd rather you didn't."

"Why is that?"

"Because it's no fun. That shit burns. How long has he been here?"

"Hard to say. When did you last see him?"

"I've never seen him, not face to face. We talked on Christmas Eve."

"On the telephone?"

"In a confessional. It's a long story."

"There's only a revolution going on, Mac.

I have all the time in the world."

"I found a contact who could lead me to the girl, Lila Hacker. I didn't trust him. I followed him to a church, and McCarl ambushed me there. He put a gun to the back of my head and forced me into a confessional. He took the priest's booth. We talked. He left. I never saw his face directly."

"And you say this was on Christmas Eve?"

"Yeah. Early in the afternoon."

I didn't tell him it happened about the same time Rico's hotel maid girlfriend was rifling my room, after seeing Marisol slink away. About the same time she took Hemingway's revolver and gave it to Rico.

It looked as if McCarl had been shot with a .38. Unfortunately, I hadn't bothered to check to see whether Hemingway's pistol had been fired when I grabbed it back from Rico.

"As I was saying," Jaime said, "it is hard to tell how long Mr. McCarl has been dead. From the bloating and the smell, I imagine it's been at least a couple of days. So I hope you can understand my curiosity as to your whereabouts. It would seem that this poor man may have been the only barrier between you and your client's daughter."

"One problem. If I killed McCarl to get to the girl two or three days ago, why am I still here? It doesn't make sense. Someone else did this to him."

"Why do I have this feeling you know who that person is?"

"I have a couple of guesses, but they wouldn't help you. You couldn't touch them if you wanted to. They're too well connected."

"There is a lot of that going around Havana right now."

He spun me around to face him. He was surprisingly strong for such a wiry little man.

"On our friendship, Mac," he said, his gaze riveted on my face. "Promise me you had nothing to do with this."

I was touched. I hadn't seen Jaime in over six years, and even then he'd given me the bum's rush out of Cuba and he'd warned me not to return any time soon, and yet he still regarded me with an affection that seemed as if we'd spent the last half decade tossing back rum together in a local whorehouse.

"I was in San Francisco de Paula, with Ernest Hemingway."

His eyebrows arched. "This is true?"

"Cross my heart. He'll vouch for me. I went over there late on Christmas Eve and I got back to the hotel an hour before you grabbed me in the lobby. We went fishing. I haven't been in Havana since three days ago. Go ahead. Call him."

Jaime glanced back at the body.

"It is not necessary. However, you said earlier you had uncovered a link to the girl, a link you did not trust. My suggestion to you is that you be very careful. It is highly likely this same person killed our unfortunate friend lying here in the alley."

"I was thinking the same thing," I said.

Chapter Twenty-Five

It was my day for visitors. Lucho Braga, the man who worked for Trafficante, was waiting next to the front desk when I returned to the Hilton. Somehow, I wasn't surprised. I saw him as I walked in the front door. I pointed toward the bar. He followed me and I ordered a couple of Hatueys before joining him at a table.

"McCarl's dead," I said.

"That's why I'm here."

"Did you kill him?"

"What do you think?"

"I think you could. I think you've done it before and you know how."

He shrugged. "I didn't kill him," he said. "I only put the zotz on guys I'm told to, and McCarl isn't important enough to my bosses. I figured you might have taken him out."

"No, but I do know who could have. I had a gun, a thirty-eight. It was taken from my room by a woman who works in the hotel and delivered to my contact here in Havana."

"Rico Gonzalez?"

That got my attention. I glared at the gangster across the table. "You've been following me?"

"Of course. Remember? Mr. Trafficante told me to keep an eye on you."

"Where's the girl?"

"I don't know. I've been following you, not Gonzalez. You think he has her?"

"He claimed to. He had the gun that was taken from my hotel room. He was in frequent contact with McCarl. My gun was a thirty-eight. McCarl was probably killed with a thirty-eight. You connect the dots."

"Sounds like Gonzalez has the Hacker girl."

"Or knows where she is. I have a deal in the works with Hacker. He's going to pay Rico and then Rico will take me to the girl and then I can take her back to Miami. I have to wait until the banks open Monday morning."

"You need some backup."

"I think Rico will be okay as long as he knows he's getting paid. The money isn't being sent here. It will be waiting for him stateside."

"Sounds like an insurance policy for you."

"I didn't intend it that way, but yeah. If I don't get the girl back to Florida, Rico doesn't get a penny."

"On the other hand, he's a drunk and he's undependable. If Rico gets the girl back to Florida, with or without you, I'd imagine Hacker would pay him off. Have you thought this through?"

"It's gotten complicated."

"I still think you need someone watching your six."

I took a long cold swig of the Hatuey. "That's not a bad idea. The police have my gun, and I don't know whether I'll get it back before blowing town. I worry that having you along could be risky. If Rico thinks one of Trafficante's men is watching him, he might get spooked and do something to the girl to shake both of us off him."

"I can do sneaky, Loame."

"Maybe we don't need sneaky. If you're in the open, Rico won't have any choice but to deal with it. And you're right. I think he would shoot his mother in the back for a hundred grand. Bringing you along would provide a lot of security. Tell you what. The banks open in Miami Monday at nine. I should hear by ten or so that Hacker has made the deposit. I'll pick you up on the way to get Rico and the girl."

I pulled his card from my wallet.

"I can reach you anytime with this number?"

"You call it and say you need me, I'll call back within five minutes. Mr. Trafficante was serious about keeping an eye on you."

"Okay. As soon as I know the money is in place, I'll give you a ring."

A bellboy entered the bar with a telephone in his hand.

"Telephone call for Mr. Loame! Mr. Cormac Loame! Telephone call for Mr. Loame!"

Braga and I exchanged glances simultaneously.

"You expecting a call?" he asked.

"No."

I waved the bellhop over and he plugged a long extension cord into a jack next to the bar.

"Excuse me," I told Braga.

It was Nelson Aquilino, in Miami.

"I thought you'd want to know," he said. "I caught up with Cecille Martinez."

Cecille Martinez, the madam over near Calle Ocho.

"She says she hasn't seen Hacker lately, say in the last year or so," Aquilino continued, "but he used to be a regular. She says he was bad news."

"He was violent?"

"Not like that. She did say he could get aggressive from time to time, but he never actually hurt anyone. She says he's weird. Goes in for strange stuff. Likes to get young girls to dress up like young boys."

"How young?"

"Cecille wouldn't tell me a lot, since there's young and then there's felony young, but I got the idea she was able to provide him with what he wanted. This other business, the dressing up like boys, I don't get."

"Go to the library. Check out a copy of that Kinsey book. I bet you'll find something about it there."

"All I'm saying is there may be something to what your boy McCarl told you. This girl you're looking for might be in trouble if you bring her back. She might be better off with McCarl."

"Not anymore. Somebody killed McCarl a couple of days ago, not long after I talked with him."

"So who's looking after the girl?"

"I'd guess the wrong guy. I hope to get her out of the country on Monday, but there's a snag."

"You're in Havana, Mac. It's the land of snags."

"I need to get someone else out of the country, too."

There was a static-laced pause on the cable line.

"Mac. You didn't."

Nelson knew all about Marisol. We'd closed several bars down over the years talking about her.

"I didn't intend to," I said. "Things happen."

"Things happen. Bullshit. There are no accidents."

"You could be right. It doesn't matter. When I leave, Marisol is coming with me. There are problems, though. The logistics are a little skewed."

"She got some boyfriend you have to sidestep?"

"Yeah, something like that."

"If it weren't for the revolution going on down there, I'd suggest getting the girl and then going back for Marisol. On the other hand, bringing the girl back to Florida doesn't sound all that smart, and I'm not at all crazy about the Marisol thing either."

"I was paid to bring the girl back. Maybe, once I get her there, I can find a way to keep Hacker off her. As for Marisol —"

I stopped and considered what rationalization best fit my motivations for bringing her back. Nothing seemed to fit.

"It doesn't matter," Nelson said. "I know you have to bring her back. Be careful."

I hung up the phone and looked at my table. Braga had disappeared, although I had a feeling he wasn't far away.

I had one more errand to run that night. It was time to take another trip to the Gonzalez compound in Miramar. Every time I visited Marisol's home, it was more dangerous. The housekeeper had already seen my face. If she got blabby around Hector, things could get violent. I hoped Marisol could keep her in line.

Hector's government car wasn't in the drive when the taxi dropped me off several doors up from the Gonzalez mansion. I chanced walking up to the front door in broad daylight. If the housekeeper answered, I'd ask to see Rico, not Marisol.

To my surprise, Rico answered the door.

"Mac!" he said, his eyes brightened by too much rum too early in the day. "I was just thinking about you!"

I grabbed him by the collar and pushed him inside the house, slamming the door behind me. I backed him up to the stairway and pinned him against the balusters.

"What did you do?" I demanded.

His face darkened and I saw the fear behind his eyes.

"What did you do?" I said again.

"I do not understand," he said, his voice raspy and strangled.

"The hell you don't. You had the handle on McCarl and the girl. Now McCarl is dead. What happened? Did he try to keep your hands off of her? Did he become useless to you, after I made your deal with Hacker? Is that why you killed him?"

Despite the fact that I had almost a half foot and seventy or eighty pounds on him, I forgot he was an athlete, trained on the jai alai *cancha* and prepared to respond with bullet-fast reflexes. He tossed up an arm, momentarily loosening my grip on his shirt, and spun away before I could reach for him again.

"Because we have been friends for so many years, I will let this pass," he said, and his voice sounded more angry than scared. "If you want the girl, do what you agreed. You have no right to come to my house and manhandle me."

"How do I know you even have the girl? I haven't seen any proof since our breakfast at the Bodeguita del Medio."

"You bring the proof of the money day after tomorrow and I'll hand her over. We can leave for Florida together. If I don't show up, I can't get the money. Is that good enough for you?"

"You don't show and the money won't matter. I'll come looking for you."

"Fair enough. Aren't you taking a risk coming here? What if my brother saw you?"

"Hector's gone. I have a feeling, after our dinner together the other evening, that he has enough to keep him busy at the Presidential Offices."

"You had dinner with my brother? How interesting."

"Did you kill McCarl?"

"Distrust is a poor foundation for a business relationship, Mac. Let us look at the positive implications of Mr. McCarl's unfortunate demise. He won't try to stop the girl's return to Florida."

"What in hell happened to you?" I asked.

"I do not understand."

"You were always lazy, but never ruthless."

"Times change. So do people. You try living under Hector's thumb for a few years. I'm tired of this. You should go. Call me tomorrow when the money is in place, and I will get the girl to you."

"I want to see Marisol."

"Why?"

"She's coming, too."

His mouth broke into a grin and he raised his hand to cover it with his fingers, but it didn't hide his laughter.

"Marisol? Escape to Florida? Whatever makes you think she will go?"

"She'll go because she has to. If she doesn't, she'll go up in flames along with Hector and the rest of the island."

"I have known my sister-in-law for a long time," Rico said. "I have found that she is difficult to sway if she has set her mind against something."

"You're saying she doesn't want to leave?"

"This is something you should discuss with her."

"Yes," Marisol said from the top of the stairwell. "I think you should discuss it with me. Leave us, Federico."

Still grinning, Rico swept at the air with his hand and retreated to the rear of the house. Marisol remained at the top of the stairs. I felt like bolting up to join her, but there was a foreboding look on her face.

"I made a mistake," she said.

"By agreeing to come to Florida?"

"I never agreed to that. My mistake was in coming to your hotel room. I gave in to my temptations and my resentments toward Hector for ignoring me. I never should have done that. I led you on."

"Come down here and talk to me."

"I'm talking to you now, as closely as I want to come to your arms. I will not fall under your spell again. Get your money from your client. Take Rico and the girl tomorrow. I must stay in Cuba."

"You can't!" I argued. "You don't understand what will happen if the reds take over the country. You won't only lose your home and your plantations. You'll lose your life!"

I couldn't stand it another minute. I dashed up the stairs, half expecting her to cower or run away. She stayed rooted in place, as if resigned to the fact that I would come to her wherever she fled and she had decided to make her stand at the top of the stairway. I grabbed her by the arms, and gazed down into her mocha eyes.

"You must listen to me," I begged.

Tears formed at the corners of her eyes and she began to tremble. I couldn't tell whether it was from fear or anger or disappointment or simply the sudden realization of the hopelessness of her situation. Whatever decision she made would mean giving up something priceless to her, and she believed I ignored that in my desire to have her for myself.

"It's not like that," I said, in anticipation of what I thought she would say next. "I know what you are losing by coming to America. I wish there was some way I could make you understand. Have you been listening to the news? The rebels are already in Santa Clara. They'll overrun your family plantations in the next day or so, scatter your workers, burn your houses there. By the first of the year they'll be in Havana. It's over, Marisol. Batista, the republic, all of it. They've already lost. You can't stay here. It's too dangerous."

As I spoke, I could feel her yielding, as if the last reserves of her denial were eroding under the relentless tide of reason. Her breathing became ragged as the tears began to cascade down her cheeks. She was torn between the only life she had ever known and her certain knowledge that her world was at an end. The only path that made sense meant starting over in a land she had never seen, by the side of the man she had believed had abandoned her six years earlier.

Even so, I could feel her body flow into mine, the soft roundness of her flesh crush against my chest. Like the country she loved, her defenses had collapsed and nothing was left except surrender.

"Monday morning," I said. "I'll come for Rico and the girl. I want you to go with us. You can fight the reds from Florida if you want, but staying here is suicide. Live to fight another day. Come to Florida."

She looked up at me, her eyes reddened, her cheeks flushed, her lips full and swollen.

"For Cuba?" she asked.

"And for me."

"For Cuba and for us," she said.

"Yes. For us. You'll come with me?"

She didn't answer directly. Instead, she threw her arms around my neck and pressed her lips against mine. They parted, and her tongue darted into my mouth to join my own. I could taste her — the saltiness of her tears, the faint aroma of the strong sweet coffee she had been drinking, and her own heady musk. It was a mélange of desire that almost made me forget the urgency of the moment. For an instant, I felt like grabbing her up and carrying her in my arms down the hall to the nearest bedroom.

"There is no other way?" she whispered.

"No," I said. "No other way."

Chapter Twenty-Six

Somehow, I got out of the house. I still don't remember how. Every moment I stayed there increased the danger that Hector would return home and find his wife in my arms. So far, I had managed to finesse Havana without killing anyone, but I knew that if Hector discovered Marisol and me together it would come down to him or me, and I had an edge on experience when it came to killing.

Marisol promised she'd come with me to Florida. I told her not to bother packing. Florida was only a half hour away by airplane and I would purchase anything she needed once we arrived. No need to arouse Hector's suspicions with loaded luggage in the closet. I told her to find her passport and any other important papers, but otherwise nothing.

My departure was marked by equal parts passion and pathos, and gallons of tears.

Back in my bed in the Havana Hilton, I stared at the ceiling fan and tried to fit together all the pieces of the complex puzzle I had forged. I had, by accident, engineered a perfect minefield. One misstep and I would be obliterated along with Lila Hacker, Rico Gonzalez, and any chance for a future for Marisol and me.

Sleep wouldn't come. If it had, I knew I'd find myself in my dreams, a boy on the ice again, paralyzed by the haunting sound of cracking like a rifle shot in the stillness.

Finally, as the first glow appeared on the horizon past the Malecòn, I found a possible solution.

I spent the next day tailing Rico, hoping he would lead me to Lila Hacker. I had rented a '37 Ford business coupe, not much more than a jalopy, but nondescript enough to blend in with many of the other poor vehicles in Habana Vieja. I parked in the sand lot next to the park across from 1472 Lagunas and watched for Rico to take off and check on his hidden paycheck.

From a protective stand of trees in the park, I watched him pull the car around and wait for Marisol to walk down the front steps of their house. I followed them to a church that looked like a junior cathedral and spied, through binoculars, as he helped her from the car. He looked jaunty, bouncing on the balls of his feet as if he were starting a round on the *cancha.* He glad-handed other parishioners like a well-oiled politician. He looked like a gambler with a dozen aces up his sleeve, and why not? He was twenty-four hours away from hitting the jackpot.

Marisol wore dark glasses, but at the solitary moment when I saw her take them off I could see her eyes were red-rimmed and her face frozen in a cast of dread. With the rebels knocking on Havana's door, she wasn't the only one, but I knew she had a different reason. I had forced her into a dead-end decision. Whether she wanted to or not, she would be leaving the country soon.

I was parked a block from the church, and I waited for over an hour for the doors to open again as the mass ended. As soon as I saw Marisol and Rico walk out, I punched the floor starter and followed them to a restaurant in the Old Town. It was obvious Rico wouldn't visit the girl with Marisol by his side. The day was turning into a bust.

An hour or so later, he drove Marisol back to the house, but he didn't get out of the car. Instead, he pulled back out onto Lagunas, and headed in the opposite direction from which he had come. I put the tail on him again.

He drove directly to the Fronton Jai Alai.

It was possible he had Lila stashed somewhere inside, but the fronton was his territory. If I barged in and ran into him, how would I explain being there?

Then it occurred to me. *Everyone* went to the Fronton Jai Alai. It was a major entertainment venue in Havana. He knew I was stuck in idle until the deposit could be made on Monday. Who could blame me for grabbing an afternoon of sport and couple of cold Hatueys while I waited?

I entered the fronton, bought a beer at the nearest bar, and scanned the grandstands. To my surprise, they were nearly full. The reds were only a two-day march from the city, and the citizens played as if nothing was wrong.

I found Rico sitting in a box a third of the way up the grandstand. He was accompanied by the doctor I'd met the previous week, and a man I didn't recognize. By his physique and by the way the girls around the box flirted with him, I figured he was a fellow player. He didn't look like a criminal, so I decided he wasn't Rico's link to Lila.

The rest of the day Rico bobbed and

weaved all over town, drinking and pressing the flesh, acting smug and self-assured.

He never led me to the girl.

I sat in my hotel room on Sunday night, listening to the radio and contemplating what I'd have for my probable last meal in Cuba, when someone knocked. Instinctively, I grabbed for my pistol, but realized my holster was still on the back of the chair, empty.

I stood to the side of the doorjamb. "Who is it?"

"Open the door, Mac," Jaime said.

I let him inside. He wasn't followed by his Cuban goon squad, so I figured the visit was friendly.

"I'm in the clear on McCarl?" I asked.

He pulled my Colt from his jacket pocket and handed it to me.

"I never doubted, of course," he said.

"Nice to know. Was McCarl killed by a thirty-eight?"

"Yes. Not yours, as it happens, which makes my job harder."

"Hell, Jaime, both of us know the case ends here. McCarl was an American gangster, and a kidnapper, for all you know. I don't see you or anyone else in Havana putting a lot of effort into solving his killing.

Not with everything else that's happening."

At first Jaime tried to glare at me, but he knew I was right, and he finally shook his head.

"I'm tired," he said.

"Join the club. You interested in dinner?"

"What did you have in mind?"

"You pick. It's your neighborhood. Let's go someplace with good food and cold drinks and some music. Let's forget about Danny McCarl and Lila Hacker and Castro and all the rest of it, and relax for an evening. With any luck, I'll be gone by this time tomorrow."

He scratched at the back of his hand, and then caught my eye.

"Promise?" he said.

We wound up in a restaurant a couple of blocks away from the hotel, a family-run place that specialized in traditional Caribe fare. Jaime ordered the oxtail pepper pot, filled with fresh thyme, garlic, cinnamon and cloves. I had Jamaican escovietch fish, wrapped in parchment paper with onions, vinegar, ackee fruit and herbs. We ordered an iced bucket of Red Stripe beer in bottles, and when it was empty we ordered another. For an evening we were common souls looking at a social disaster in the making from different sides of the conflict.

As we ate, I told Jaime about the deal Rico had forged to turn the girl over. I withheld my suspicions that Rico might have been responsible for McCarl's murder.

Halfway through the second bucket of beer, I decided it was time to stop dancing around the issue. "Something Hemingway told me the other night worries me," I said. "Once the reds take over, there are going to be a lot of badges up against the wall at La Cabana. Castro will install his own law enforcement and there won't be room for many old guard Batista-era officers."

"It's not the first time I've heard this, Mac."

"I'm leaving tomorrow. As soon as Rico gets his money, he'll deliver the girl and I'll take her, Rico and Marisol to Florida. Why don't you come with us?"

He opened a new bottle of Red Stripe, and took a long drag from it. "You are suggesting that I desert my post? In the middle of a revolution?"

"Yes. Live to fight another day."

"It's tempting," he said. "But let me ask you this. Suppose the tables were turned. Let us say that Russians invaded the United States from Canada and were marching their way toward Washington. Given the opportunity, would you escape to save your own life?"

"I'd consider it, at least."

"So you were drafted in World War II."

"Hell, no. I volunteered the day after Pearl Harbor."

"You were in college at the time. You could have gotten a deferment."

He was right. I didn't have to go to Europe and dodge bullets for three years. Nobody had a gun to my head and I wasn't conscripted. I could have remained in Georgia, stayed in college, graduated, then could have enlisted as an officer. Instead, I spent three years as a grunt, slogging through the mud of Italy and Sicily and sweating out the blast furnace of the sands of Tunisia, collecting an interesting array of scars from shrapnel, ricochets and near misses.

"No deal, huh?" I said.

"Thanks for asking," Jaime said. "I could go to Florida, but could I look myself in the mirror afterward, knowing I had saved myself but left so many of my friends to an uncertain fate?"

"I had to ask. If the country falls, keep your head down, okay?"

"That you can depend on. Now, enough of this talk. I know a place a couple of blocks from here that has the most marvelous salsa music."

The telephone call came at ten o'clock the next morning. I was shaved, showered and dressed. My bags were packed, but I had kept my pistol out and it sat comfortably in my shoulder holster under my linen jacket. It was nice to have it back. I wondered whether I'd need it before day's end.

The international operator connected Hacker.

"Did you make the arrangements?" I asked.

"Yes. There's a bank account at the Miami National Bank in the name of Federico Gonzalez. I've deposited a hundred thousand in it."

"Miami National? Isn't it owned by Lansky and the Teamsters?"

"Yes. It's safe, though. Who's gonna rob a bank owned by Lansky and the Teamsters? Where in hell would they hide?"

"Good point. Okay. I need proof."

"I've already wired confirmation to your hotel. It should be at the front desk shortly."

"All right, then. I'll contact Mr. Gonzalez, and go pick up your daughter."

"You bring her home safe, Loame. I'll make it worth your effort."

"I'll call you when we're on the way."

"You did good work. I won't forget it."

I racked the telephone and allowed myself to sink into the chair next to the window.

"No," I said to the absent Hacker, after a few seconds. "No, you won't forget it."

I dialed the Gonzalez house and, in a disguised voice, asked for Rico.

"It's done," I told him. "A hundred thousand in the Miami National Bank, in your name. Hacker's wired the confirmation to the hotel. I should have it in a few minutes."

"You have made me happy, Mac. I know this has placed a strain on our friendship, but I came through for you, did I not?"

"Sure," I said. "You've been stand-up. Bring Marisol with you when you bring the girl. Make any excuse to Hector you need to. By dinner we'll be in Miami, and he won't be able to touch us."

There was a brief silence. Then Rico said, "I don't think it is safe to bring Marisol and the girl to the Hilton. Hector already knows you are staying there. I suggest we meet somewhere else and proceed to the airport from there."

"Where?"

"The Bodeguita del Medio is a good place. Out of the way and you know how to get there, right?"

"Of course. I met you there last Friday."

"Yes. Bring the confirmation telegram from Hacker. The girl, my sister-in-law and I will be waiting there for you."

"I'll see you around noon. We'll grab the first plane out of José Martí this afternoon. Don't screw this up, Rico. Too much is riding on it. No girl, no money."

I made one more telephone call, to the number on the card Braga had given me. I was a little surprised when he answered it himself.

"It's set. I'm supposed to meet them at Bodeguita del Medio. You know the place?"

"Sure."

"How do you want to do this?"

"Take a taxi," he said, and he gave me an address. "We'll take a car I have here. Rico won't dare cross you if I'm there. One or the other of us would make him very sorry."

I told him I'd be there in a half hour.

I rechecked the room to make sure I hadn't forgotten anything and then toted my bag down to the lobby. The desk clerk took a moment to find Hacker's cablegram and then handed it across the desk as I slid him my keys.

"We are checking out, Señor Loame?" he asked.

"Yes," I said. "My business in Havana is

about wrapped up."

He totaled up the check and I handed him enough pesos to cover the bill and leave a little for his discretion. He nodded appreciatively.

"I'll need a taxi," I said.

"To the airport?"

"No. I have to make a stop before heading to José Martí. I have one last bit of business to attend to."

"Of course."

He called the concierge over. "This is Señor Loame," he announced, perhaps a little too formally. "Señor Loame requires a taxi. Could you attend to it, please?"

"Immediately," the concierge replied.

I followed him to the front entrance, where he asked me to wait while he arranged for a cab. It took a couple of minutes, during which I once again ran through all the details I'd need to complete before the day was out. While I was no fan of the mobs, for once I was going to be grateful to have a gangster riding alongside me for protection. I had a feeling that Braga, despite his slight appearance, could prove to be a formidable opponent if the situation went south and guns started blazing.

Finally, the concierge walked back into the lobby. "Your taxi is waiting," he said.

I slipped the concierge a couple of pesos for his trouble, loaded my suitcase into the trunk of the taxi, and took a seat. I gave the driver the address Braga had provided.

"Si," he said as he started the cab.

As he pulled away from the curb, I tried to memorize as much of the passing scenery as I could. In all likelihood, this would be my last trip to Cuba for a long time. Batista's regime had lasted almost six years. The US government had little patience with communists, and every indication was that Castro and his buddies were going to go all bolshie on the island. It was even possible that my country might embargo Cuba entirely. If that happened, nobody was getting in or out, which meant that Marisol would have lost her homeland.

The driver pulled up in front of a stone building with ornate wrought-iron gates and bars on the windows. He pulled the car out of gear and set the parking brake.

"What is this place?" I asked.

The driver turned and pointed a huge Tokarev automatic in my face. I started to reach for my pistol, but he shoved the automatic even closer.

"You get out now," the driver said. "No pay. Just get out."

I opened the door, and stepped out to the

curb. My first impression was that he was robbing me. With the whole island going to hell, it made sense that some jokers would try to profit from the chaos. He started to drive off. I pulled my pistol, in some sort of futile gesture of defiance. He rounded a corner before I could get a shot off.

"Fuck me!" I shouted, mostly to whatever fates continued to conspire against me.

As I did, two massive wooden doors set into the front of the building opened and four soldiers marched out. The man in front wore a close-fitting uniform with shoulder braids, and a peaked cap with a Cuban crest front and center. The other solders wore fatigues with bright white woven canvas belts, and helmets. All of them were armed. I know when I'm outgunned. I holstered my Colt. The day had disintegrated into chaos, and I wondered just how bad things could get.

The man in the peaked hat stepped forward. "Cormac Loame?"

"Yes."

"You will come with us."

"Wait," I said. "What's this about?"

"No questions. You will come with us."

"The hell I will. I demand to speak with someone from the US embassy."

"Sadly, they are otherwise engaged. Step

this way."

He started to step aside. I had to decide what to do. Running was an option, but it was a hundred feet easy to the next corner and I wouldn't get halfway before taking two or three rifle rounds in the back. Going along willingly presented other complications. I'd heard stories of what happened to people who disappeared off the streets of Havana and I didn't like the way they ended.

It dawned on me that I had been sold out. Rico must have decided that a hundred thousand in a Miami bank was chump change. He probably planned to take the girl to Florida himself, shake Hacker down for more money, maybe a lot more money.

Rico was an idiot. Obviously, he didn't realize that if he tried to extort money from Hacker, he'd wind up as shark chum in the Bahamas. That didn't help me at the moment, though. I was trapped, and needed to decide what to do right away.

I waited too long. Something hard and heavy bashed me behind my knees, dropping me to the sidewalk. I tried to brace myself with my arms, but then I took another whack across the kidneys, the kind of blow that would have me pissing blood for a week. It cut all my strings. I rolled over into a fetal position on the sidewalk and the last thing I recall was being picked up by the soldiers and dragged through the massive wooden doors, before I passed out from the pain.

Chapter Twenty-Seven

I wasn't out for long. It's possible I never completely lost consciousness. You can go to a place so full of pain that nothing else exists, not even time.

After a while, I don't know how long, the mists in front of my eyes began to part and I found myself sitting in a wooden chair in the middle of a shabby office. My wrists were handcuffed to the arms of the chair. My jacket was gone, as was my shoulder rig and my .38.

The only sound was the incessant ticking of a clock on the wall. I glanced at it. One-fifteen. I had left the hotel around ten-thirty. The cab ride had taken at most ten minutes, so I had been out for a little over two hours. I could feel the muscles in the middle of my back spasm and clench, and I knew without looking that I was going to have a hell of a bruise.

I couldn't figure out what had happened.

The taxi driver was clearly a plant, I got that much. The concierge must have been in on the sellout. Maybe the desk clerk, too. But I couldn't understand where I was and why. This level of duplicity seemed beyond Rico's pull.

Time passed. At one-forty I heard boot steps coming up the hallway, then the rasp of a key in the door's lock. I couldn't turn my head around far enough to see the door, but I heard someone walk in and then the sound of the door slamming shut. Someone stood behind me. I could hear him breathing.

Finally, the man stepped around into my line of sight. It was the soldier with the peaked cap. He took it off and placed it on his desk, then pulled calfskin gloves off and laid them next to the cap.

"My name is Colonel Raul Machado," he said. "You are in the headquarters of the *Servicio de Inteligencia Militar.*"

"I've heard of you," I said, and noted my mouth didn't seem to want to work correctly. Had I been slapped around while I was out? "You're the Cuban secret police. You do Batista's dirty work for him. You make people disappear. You put people he doesn't like up against the wall at La Cabana fortress."

Machado leaned against the desk and braced himself with one hand as he stroked his mustache with the other.

"This much is true," he said at last. "The SIM has done many unsavory things. Do you know why you are here?"

"Not a clue. It seems ever since I got to Havana I've made enemies out of one thug or another. Join the club."

Machado glanced at the clock over his desk. "Almost one forty-five. My daughter is in a piano recital at her school in an hour. I should be there to support her. Why do you think I am here?"

My sore stomach clenched. I felt nauseous. Everything was turning to shit.

"I don't know! I'm from Miami, just here to do a job! I'm not political. I have nothing to do with anything going on in Cuba! I want to see someone from the American consulate."

He ignored me, picked up a folder from his desk, and flipped through it. "You arrived in Havana several days ago, carrying a weapon."

"Sure I did. So what? It cleared customs. I always bring a gun to Cuba."

"Why?"

"It's a dangerous place." As if to prove my

point, I pointed at my restraints with my chin.

"Within three hours of your arrival, you visited a *bodega* owned by a family named Escobar. What was your business there?"

"I had worked with the old man Escobar before. I'm not from Cuba. I live in the United States. When I come to Havana, it helps to have help from people who are here all the time."

"You contacted this man Escobar before you left Florida?"

"No."

"How did you know he was still here?"

"I knew where he had been before, so I went there. I didn't know until I got there that he was dying."

"And now he is dead?"

"That's what I heard the other day."

"From whom did you hear this?"

"Jaime Guzman. He's a detective with the Havana police. Call him. He'll tell you I'm okay."

"We will discuss that later. From the Escobar residence, you went to El Floridita."

"Have you had a tail on me all along?"

"Please, I will ask the questions. Why did you go to El Floridita?"

"Escobar's kid told me I could meet a man there who could help me."

"Did you meet this man?"
"Yeah. His name was Luis Gopaldo."
"Señor Gopaldo is dead, is he not?"
"You already know he is. He was shot at the marina the night after I met with him at El Floridita. What in hell is this about?"
"These are routine questions."
"Do you always assault Americans and chain them to a chair to ask routine questions?"
"When it seems appropriate. Tell me everything you know about the Twenty-Sixth of July Movement."
"The rebels? All I know about them is what's on the news."
"Is that so? In that case, Mr. Loame, I must apologize. Obviously there has been a great miscarriage of justice here."
"No problem. Cut me loose, give me back my belongings, and I'll be on my way. I'm on a tight schedule."
Of course, I knew he had no intention of doing any of those things. At some level, I may have just been buying time.
"First, I would like to ask you a question. Perhaps you will appreciate the irony of your situation. You say you always bring weapons into Cuba, which may or may not be understandable. Do you not find it coincidental that, within hours of your ar-

rival, you managed to make contact with a suspected agent of the Twenty-Sixth of July Movement?"

"Old Escobar? He couldn't be an agent of anything. He was delirious."

"Not him. The young man. His son."

"If that kid represents the rebels, Batista has nothing to worry about. The kid was a goofball."

"A goof . . . ball?" Machado raised one eyebrow.

"A lamebrain. Not very smart."

"And yet we have every reason to believe he has been offering aid and assistance to soldiers who wish to bring down Cuba's legitimate government. But allow me to continue. Only an hour or two after meeting with young Escobar, you somehow managed to contact yet another suspected agent."

"Luis Gopaldo?"

"So you know about his activities?"

"Of course not. I never heard of Gopaldo until I went to see old Escobar. The kid sent me to him."

"Why?"

"Like I said, Escobar was dying. The kid said Gopaldo might have information that could help me."

"Help you to do what?"

"My job! I was hired by a man in Miami to find his daughter here in Cuba."

"And have you found her?"

"More or less. I have a contact who knows where she is. He's willing to hand her over for a price. I arranged with my client to pay that price this morning. Did you have Gopaldo killed?"

"Why do you ask?"

"Loose ends. They annoy me."

"Luis Gopaldo was an enemy of the state. We were not following you, Mr. Loame. We were following *him.* Had he lived, Señor Gopaldo would have earned a short visit to La Cabana fortress in due time."

"Gopaldo was working for the Gonzalez family. Hector Gonzalez is one of Batista's closest advisors. You think Gopaldo was also working with the rebels? It doesn't play."

"We have found rebel infiltration at many levels of the government. Sympathizers are everywhere."

"Kind of makes you wonder whether you're on the right side, doesn't it?"

"There is a saying, Señor Loame. 'History is written by the victors.' In time, we will all know who was on the right side."

"And what about Hector Gonzalez? Do you suspect him?"

"No," someone said from behind

Machado. I hadn't heard anyone else walk down the hallway, and I hadn't been aware there was another person in the room. Now I heard footsteps as the third man walked toward me.

I didn't need to see him to know who he was. I would have known his voice anywhere.

Hector Gonzalez circled the chair and looked down at me.

"I am not a suspect," he said. "Now, perhaps you would like to explain why you were at my home last evening."

Chapter Twenty-Eight

"If you know I was there," I said, "you also know I met with your brother. I've had several meetings with Rico over the last several days. He knows where the girl is."

"Is that so?" Hector asked. "I find that convenient. You come all the way to Havana to find a missing girl, and your best lead comes from my brother?"

"You can ask him if you want. He wants money from my client to move to Florida and make a fresh start after the revolution."

"Rico is foolish. There will be no revolution. We've held the rebels at Santa Clara, and in a short time the army will have dispatched them."

"You believe that, Hector? Did Batista tell you that to reassure you? Let me ask you something. Luis Gopaldo worked for your family. Rico is convinced the revolution will take place. He has to be getting his inside dope from someone. Answer me, and answer me truthfully. Did you kill Gopaldo?"

Hector glanced at Machado, who seemed more amused by the conversation than concerned. Then Hector said, "No. I did not kill him. Gopaldo was useful to me. He helped to keep down *disturbances* on the plantations. He also assembled information on my enemies."

"And I thought *I* was your only real enemy," I said, my voice filled with sarcasm.

"To be truthful, since we are telling the truth here, Loame, I have not thought of you in years."

"Not since I gave up writing to Marisol. You intercepted those letters, didn't you?"

"Yes. Even in nineteen fifty-two, I had access to certain information and resources. I had her mail confiscated, destroyed your letters, and let the rest through."

"That's what I figured. Colonel, you didn't have Gopaldo killed, did you?"

Hector and I both looked to Machado. He shook his head and said, "I was deprived of that privilege. We are keeping a close eye on young Escobar, however."

I turned my attention back to Hector. "I think I'm beginning to figure this out. Ever since Jaime Guzman told me Gopaldo was murdered, I figured you for it. After he was killed, I learned that Gopaldo worked for you and I presumed you had discovered he was moonlighting for me and you killed him for it. You say you didn't kill Gopaldo, and the colonel didn't have him killed, so I have to wonder who did."

"Perhaps his rebel coconspirators," Machado suggested.

"It's possible, but I don't think so. Gopaldo knew I was looking for the girl. What are the chances he told Rico? Rico believes the reds are going to take over the island, probably because of inside tips he got from Gopaldo, and he's been looking for an escape route should the island fall. Rico came to me before Christmas and told me he had found the girl. Said he had contacts he could exploit that I couldn't. I don't believe that. Gopaldo, I could see, but not Rico. Rico's a playboy and a womanizer, but he's also lazy. Am I right, Hector?"

"Yes," he said, reluctantly.

"So, this is what I think happened. I hired Gopaldo, on young Escobar's recommendation, to help find the girl. I can easily believe that Gopaldo had lowlife friends. My guess is that Gopaldo found the girl and McCarl within hours of the time I hired him. But he decided to string me along for a while, get some more money out of me. His mistake was taking Rico into his confidence.

"Rico saw his way off the island. He got Gopaldo to tell him how to contact Lila Hacker, and he decided he could make his stake for a fresh start in Florida by selling her to me. He contacted me at the Riviera to set up a reunion, but he couldn't come out and say he had the girl. How could he explain knowing that I was looking for her? So, instead, he staged this cobbled-up meeting at the Fronton Jai Alai and allowed me to give him a picture of Lila Hacker. That way, he could play the hero by doing me a favor and *finding* her.

"Gopaldo must have discovered that Rico was planning to double-cross him. Somehow, Gopaldo and Rico wound up down at the marina and Rico killed Gopaldo to avoid losing his reward. After waiting a day or so, he contacted me with this story about how he had found the girl by using his nonexistent underground contacts. After I made the deal with him to deliver the girl, McCarl was murdered. That way Rico removed the last line of resistance to returning the girl to Miami. He killed Gopaldo *and* McCarl. Did your family proud, Hector."

Hector pulled a chair from beside Machado's desk and sat a few feet from me. "Why were you at my home last night?"

"As I said, my client in Miami approved

the payoff. I had to work out the arrangements with Rico to make the transfer — the money for the girl."

"How did you plan to do it?"

"My client made a deposit this morning in Rico's stateside bank account. There's a cablegram in my jacket, wherever you've put it, confirming a bank deposit in Miami in his name. As soon as Rico gets the confirmation, he takes me to the girl and I get off the island. I was heading out to meet him when I was abducted by Machado's soldiers."

I didn't mention Lucho Braga. Somehow, I felt that invoking gangsters wouldn't help my case. Besides, I wasn't completely certain that Braga hadn't sold me out himself.

"What will Rico do in America?"

"Beats me. I presume he has some plan in place. Maybe he's going to make jai alai the next national sport. Gopaldo might have been tied in with the reds somehow, but I think Rico's out for Rico. I don't see him thriving under a commie regime."

Hector turned to Machado. "Colonel?"

Machado settled into his own chair and tapped his chin a couple of times. He seemed to be making a decision.

"I am satisfied Señor Loame is not involved with the insurrectionists," he finally said. "According to you, he has been in Florida since before Fulgencio reacquired the presidency, and he has been back in Havana for less than a week. I do not see him as a security risk. What would you like me to do?"

I should have been reassured by Colonel Machado, but I also knew that I might not have helped my chances much. Rico was slime, but he was also Hector's brother. It was possible I was no longer a target for the Cuban secret police, but who knew what Hector might do to protect Rico?

"I need to talk with my brother about this," Hector said. "If Loame is right, I will have to decide what to do about my brother."

"That has nothing to do with me," I said. "Make him hand over the girl and I'm back in Florida before you know it."

Along with Marisol, I thought.

"I can't take that chance. Colonel, can I assume that — if Federico killed Luis Gopaldo — he would be considered a hero for putting down a rebel conspirator?"

"I would not hold a grudge against him for it. I certainly wouldn't consider it a state security matter. Murder, however, is still a crime in Cuba."

"This wouldn't be considered murder. It would be a wartime casualty."

"And this Señor McCarl? Another wartime casualty?"

"That is for lawyers to decide."

Hector, his eyes suddenly tired, furrowed his brow. He rubbed at his temples as if trying to make a momentous decision. After a minute or two, he slapped his thighs with his palms in something resembling finality.

"You can hold Loame on suspicion?" he asked Machado.

"Of course I can. I do not choose to do so."

"Why is that?"

"After talking with him, I do not suspect him of any crime against the state."

"I cannot have him running around loose. I need time to talk with my brother and decide what we will do."

"Well, he was brought here by one of our agents driving a taxicab," Machado said. "Loame has no transportation. It would be rude to make him walk — wherever he is going."

I had to hand it to Hector. He was sharp and he was quick.

"I have facilities at my plantation outside Matanzas," he said. "Perhaps you could transport him there?"

Machado checked the clock. It was five minutes after two. He risked being late for his daughter's recital. "In the interest of getting back to my family," he said, "I will be happy to make these arrangements."

Chapter Twenty-Nine

As prisons went, it wasn't all that bad.

A detail of Machado's officers placed me in the backseat of a black government Ford and positioned themselves on each side to assure I wouldn't bolt. Then we took a drive through the seaside jungles for about an hour. We arrived at a sugarcane plantation not long before sunset. There I was half led, half dragged to a small outbuilding, and tossed unceremoniously inside, where I landed on the dirt floor in a cloud of dust.

I realized that this had been some kind of worker's hut. About four feet up from the floor, there was a long window that was only about six inches high — far too small for me to climb through. I could see through it, however, and it did provide some cross ventilation, which kept the room from becoming a sweat lodge. I was glad it was almost New Year's Eve. I'd have hated to be in the hovel in the heat of summer.

There wasn't much to see through the window, except for acres of sugarcane, some electrical poles with power lines, and a long dirt road that converged in the distance to a single vanishing point.

I tested the door, which didn't budge. For better or worse, I wasn't going anywhere for a while. I sat on the musty, mildewed cot, and listened to the night come alive outside the hut.

I thought something would happen quickly, but the hours dragged on. For some reason, the mosquitoes avoided the inside of the hut. The temperature cooled down and by midnight I needed the coarse wool blanket on the bed. Shortly after that, I fell asleep.

Not long after sunrise, the door opened, and a young boy — five or six years old — carried in a tray of bread and butter and some grilled peppers and onions wrapped in Cuban tortillas, along with a tin pot full of hot black coffee. I was starving so I gobbled the food. Then I tested the door. It was locked again. Hector wasn't taking any chances.

As soon as I tried to force the door, I heard a rattle on the other side, which I presumed to be a padlock, followed by the sound of a hasp being thrown. The door opened and a man pointed a World War I–vintage Enfield bolt-action rifle at me. He wasn't one of Machado's soldiers. He was dressed in the typical cotton shirt and trousers you'd expect to find on a Cuban sugar-plantation worker, and he wore a wide-brimmed straw hat. His feet were bare. Obviously, Hector had sent word ahead that I was to be held, but Machado wasn't willing to waste two armed men to do the job.

I showed the man both of my hands, to demonstrate that I had no weapons and didn't plan to attack him. He nodded and closed the door. I heard the hasp reattached and the click of the padlock.

I sighed, thinking it could be worse. There was the bed in one corner, which hadn't been terribly uncomfortable considering it probably had been constructed before the Spanish-American War. There were a couple of chairs and a small table. I didn't hear the man with the Enfield walk away, so I had to presume he stood guard outside the door.

I spent two days in a Cuban-plantation version of solitary confinement. I didn't have much to do to pass the time, except look out the window and contemplate what other kind of mischief — or perhaps mayhem — Hector had in store for me.

I hadn't come to Cuba to solve a murder,

or even to become a bit player in one, but that was the way things always seemed to happen on the island. What worried me was what might be happening to Lila Hacker while I languished in my plantation hovel. If my theory was right, Rico had killed Gopaldo in order to use Lila to get Cecil Hacker's money, and then had killed McCarl to prevent him from interfering with his plans. Without Lila and Danny McCarl to confirm that Rico had brought them together with me, his motive for Gopaldo's murder disappeared.

I wouldn't put it past Hector to force Rico to produce Lila, and then either do away with her or ship her off to Florida under coercion, in order to keep her from testifying against Rico should the case be prosecuted at some point — presuming, of course, that she even knew Rico had killed McCarl. I knew Hector wouldn't roll over on his own brother, but Machado also knew what Rico had done, and after giving it a lot of thought I had come to the conclusion that — ruthless or not — Machado had a sense of honor and duty that might trigger him into turning Rico over to the authorities.

If Hacker was abusing his daughter, it would put Lila in peril, but I had Nelson

Aquilino looking into that and I was sure that he — having daughters himself — would take over McCarl's role as her protector, at least until I could get back to handle the job myself.

If I got back. Hector hadn't turned me into sugarcane fertilizer so far, but it wasn't yet out of the question.

That evening, along with the boy who brought me my food, a young girl brought a fresh bucket of water and a couple of washrags, which I used to clean myself as best as I could. The next morning, along with the food and the washing materials, she brought a change of clothes — the traditional cotton guayabera work shirt and trousers — and took my now-filthy shirt and pants with her. That evening, she returned my clothes, carefully washed and folded.

On the third morning, I'd had enough. Every time the doors opened, I had tried to glance out to see how many men might be watching the hut, and how they were armed. I had come to the conclusion that — most of the time — there was one man. I had heard conversations in Spanish outside the door on occasion, but that seemed to be when one man or another was being relieved of watch duty.

The fact that the guard was using an Enfield rifle was encouraging. Being a bolt-action weapon, he would only have time to squeeze off one shot before I could subdue him. If I planned it right, I could be pretty sure that shot wouldn't end up in my ass. It would probably arouse any other guards Hector had put on me, though, so I had to be prepared to run to the jungle and try to lose myself in the undergrowth there.

I waited patiently until I heard footsteps approach. I didn't have a weapon, but I did have a foot of height and sixty pounds on the little brown guy with the Enfield, so I figured I could overwhelm him easily, if I could surprise him.

As it had before, the door rattled, accompanied by the metallic sound of the key in the padlock. A few seconds later, the door swung open and I leapt toward the guard.

I missed him by almost half a foot, as he deftly sidestepped my attack, and he wasn't the guard who had been standing outside my hut.

"Really?" Lucho Braga looked down at me, sprawled on the ground. "That's the best you can do? Nice place you got here. Tired of it yet?"

"You bet. We have to get to Havana, find Rico and the girl —"

"Whoa, Loame. It's okay. Things have

happened while you were meditating here in the jungle. The game's changed a little. Follow me."

He led me up a dirt plantation road to the boundaries of the main house, where the landscape slowly transformed from wild, untamed vines and brambles to a carefully tended garden. As we walked, I tried to make all the connections. Braga worked with Trafficante, who was tangentially connected with Sam Giancana in Chicago and the Bonnano family in New York. All of the mobs were intertwined with Batista and, by extension, Hector Gonzalez. I couldn't help wondering whether Braga might have jumped the fence, at his boss's order, and was walking me into a killing field.

When we reached the back of the plantation house, Braga led me up to a screened gallery and into the house itself. We walked down a short hallway and turned into a parlor.

Hector was waiting there for us. So were Rico, Marisol and Lila Hacker.

Lila didn't look like Veronica Lake anymore. Without her makeup, she looked more like a frightened, disheveled fourteen-year-old girl, her cheeks tear-streaked, her hair limp and greasy from neglect.

"Have a seat, Loame," Hector said.

I ignored him, and walked over to Lila. Kneeling beside her chair, I said, "Are you all right?"

She nodded and made a small, fear-filled grunting sound.

"I've been sent to find you," I told her. "Don't worry. Everything's going to work out."

"Don't make me go home," she said, her voice higher than I expected and her tone pitiful.

I patted her hand and turned to face Hector.

"Summit meeting?" I said, gesturing toward the others in the room.

"You place me in an uncomfortable position," Hector said. "Against my better instincts, I find that I am forced to trust you."

That was surprising. But I'm supposed to be a tough guy, so I tried not to let it show.

"You could do worse," I told him. "What's happened?"

"The government has suffered an unfortunate turn of events."

"Castro and his buddies have kicked Batista's ass," Braga explained.

Hector winced. The calm, self-assured man with whom I had shared dinner had disappeared. He was still physically formidable, but his face wore a lost look. His eyes were the eyes of a mystified man, faced with the destruction of the world he had come to accept as eternal.

"It seems the rebels will win for now," he said. "If I am to salvage what little I can of holdings, I cannot be distracted by familial matters. There will be time for that later."

He glanced over at Rico and his meaning was clear. Rico's face was swollen and he couldn't look me in the eye. He had the appearance of a child who'd been beaten often and severely. He was Hector's brother, but my dealings with Hector had left me with no doubt that, if needed, he would rough up his brother, especially if he believed Rico had done something to sully the family honor. If I was right, Rico had done more than his share of sullying.

"I need to get Marisol out of the country," Hector continued. "It is not safe for her here. Mr. Braga was sent to me by Mr. Trafficante. He confirmed much of the story you told me. I made inquiries of my brother." He glared at Rico again, and I could almost see my old friend crumple and collapse inside.

"He led you to the girl," I finished.

"Yes."

"I suppose he told you everything," I said,

not daring to glance at Marisol. Rico was unscrupulous. I was certain he'd sold me out in an attempt to save his own skin.

"About the girl, yes. He confirmed he had made a deal with you to return the girl for money from her father."

"And the killings?"

For a moment, Hector ignored the question. Then his shoulders slumped. "There are things one doesn't wish to know about a family member, Loame. Whatever Rico has done, it is an act he will have to carry in his own conscience. Based on what he has told me, there is no future for him in Cuba. He will be safe from the law in Florida. Here, he would be a distraction."

Now I did catch Marisol's eye. She nodded. Even though Hector might have suspected something, he had no concrete knowledge of her infidelity or our plans. Rico had kept at least one secret.

"So," Hector said, "I need to ask for your help. Marisol would not be safe in Cuba. I do not believe my brother would be of any use in defending our country even if that might restore his honor. You want the girl. Here she is. Take her back to Florida, but — also — take Marisol and Rico. I am aware of your capabilities, Loame. I believe you can guarantee their safe passage. With

Mr. Braga's help, of course."

"Mr. Trafficante wanted me to keep you safe," Braga said to me. "When you didn't show on Monday, I figured you'd been double-crossed. I started looking for you. It was Hector who contacted Mr. Trafficante to confirm your story about coming to Havana to find Hacker's daughter. Mr. Trafficante wants me to help you get out of the country."

"There is little time," Hector said. "The panic has begun in Havana. Already people are lining up at the airport, desperate to board any plane leaving the country. You must hurry. Take the girl, take Marisol and Rico, and get back to Florida as quickly as possible. You may have hours, no more than a day. I have other matters to which I must attend."

I crossed the room to Braga. "Can Traffi-cante get us onto a plane out of Marti?"

"I don't think so," he said. "Mr. Traffi-cante believes he can make a deal with Castro and Che, so he's not bugging out. The rest of them are loading everything they can onto every available plane. I don't have any pull with the other families in Cuba. We're on our own."

"What about boats?"

"When I left Havana, the marina was

emptying out, mostly Americans heading back to the States. There might be some fishing boats left, but whether they can get across the Florida Straits —" He shrugged.

"You know anyone with a small plane, perhaps at one of the fields away from the city?"

"No. The reds control everything south of the city now. Maybe to the west we can find an airfield they haven't reached."

"Don't bother," I said. "I know someone with a boat."

I gently grasped Lila Hacker's elbow. She hadn't said much since I'd come into the room. Rico already had a leather valise in hand. Marisol sat in the chair next to a suitcase. She stared at the floor.

"If we're going, we need to leave now," I said.

"Then why are we waiting?" Rico whined. His eyes were dilated. He was jumpy. If I hadn't known better, I'd have thought he was wired on bennies.

Hector pulled Marisol to her feet, and stroked her arms as he looked down on her upturned face. "I have not been the husband you might have wanted," he said. "I have been ambitious. I have neglected you. I did not see at the time what I had. Now that all seems lost, I know what a waste I have made of our time together. I hope you will forgive me. Go to Florida. Wait for me. We will drive these rebels out and I will come to bring you home again. Will you? Will you wait for me?"

She didn't say anything. Instead, she leaned and rested her cheek on his chest. I could see the furrow her tears had cut on her face. She nodded twice.

"You will not be foolish," she said to him. "Do not take unnecessary chances."

"This is our home. I will do what I must to protect it. Have no fear, *cara.* I will survive this and I will come for you."

He allowed her to remain in his arms for another few minutes and then his face hardened. He opened a writing desk and handed me my shoulder holster and Colt automatic. "Protect, them, Loame. What has happened between us in the past is irrelevant. This is a debt of honor."

We piled into a two-tone Packard Clipper that Braga had waiting outside the front gallery. At the last minute Hector pulled Braga aside. From inside the car, I watched them have an intense conversation on the veranda. Hector shook Braga's hand and waved him away.

Braga took the wheel, and I rode shotgun.

Rico and Marisol sat on the backseat, sandwiching Lila between them.

"What was that?" I asked Braga as we pulled away from the house.

"What?"

"You and Hector."

"Business. Nothing you need to worry about. Where to, Loame?"

"San Francisco de Paula. You know it?"

"I can get there, if we don't run into rebel patrols first."

He knew a way that bypassed the city, comprised of mostly washboard dirt roads and plantation trails. Once or twice, as we rounded mountain bends, I could look down and see Havana. There were dozens of plumes of smoke rising from the city, as if the people had set bonfires in every square. I realized it was the fingerprint of riots, people destroying the very home they should have been trying to protect in their zeal to escape the invaders from the south.

After what seemed like hours, we broke through an opening in the jungle and swung downhill into San Francisco de Paula. I directed Braga to *Finca Vigia.*

"This is Hemingway's place," he said, as he jerked the car to a stop on the road in front of the house.

"You've been here?"

"I drove Trafficante out here once or twice for parties. Mr. Hemingway likes parties. You know him?"

"We've met. I spent Christmas fishing with him. It's a long story. Let's go."

We piled out of the Packard. I led us up the path to the door, dodging a couple of cats along the way. I could hear movement inside. The door opened when I banged on it, and Hemingway peered out.

"Hey, Loame. Got the girl, did you?"

"Yes, and now we need help."

He led us into the main room. Lila had no idea who Hemingway was, but she was transfixed by the mounted animal heads on the wall. Rico and Marisol stared at the author, amazed. Braga stood by the door and looked bored, but I could tell that nothing in the room escaped his notice.

"Tell me everything," Hemingway said.

"There's not much to tell. I found the girl with the help of Mr. Braga over there by the door."

Hemingway shot a glance at Marisol. "And this is your paramour?"

I took Marisol's hand and walked her over to him. "Marisol Gonzalez," I said. "Mr. Hemingway."

"So lovely," Hemingway said as he grasped her hand. For a moment, I thought he'd kiss it. "I understand now, Loame. Yes. Well worth the effort. Heard the news? Looks bad for the regime."

"That's why we're here. The airports are swamped. We can't get a plane. I need to ask if you'll take us to Florida on the *Pilar.*"

His face clouded and he stroked his grizzled chin. "No. Can't. Simply can't. Miss the revolution? I'd sooner shoot myself. No, Loame, I'm not going to Florida."

"We have to get off the island," I said. "We need a boat. You're our best shot."

"Out of the question. I'm staying here to ride this thing out. However —"

I waited as he appeared to run through options in his increasingly clouded head.

"What?" I finally asked.

"Well, *Pilar* doesn't give a damn if she's here or not, does she?"

"You'd give us the boat?"

"Lend it, more precisely. I'd want it back, of course."

"Damn it! We can't come back, once we get to Florida!"

"Yes. I can see that. You'd need a captain. Someone who could come back without problems. I think we can work this out. In fact, I may have the perfect person. Give me a few moments."

He lumbered out of the room toward the

guesthouse.

"Old guy's pickled," Braga said from the front door.

"I agree," Rico said. "Are you sure we can trust him?"

"Is there a choice?" I said. "He has a boat. We need a boat. Let's clear one hurdle at a time."

Hemingway reappeared with a sallow, bloated man whose salt-and-pepper hair was still tousled from his pillow. The man's eyes were bleary and his gait unsteady, but there was something familiar about his face.

"My houseguest," Hemingway announced. "And a sailing man to boot. Been on a bender, I'm afraid, but who among us hasn't lately? He'll get the job done for you, though. Say hello to Mr. Allan Sanders."

Chapter Thirty

For a moment, nobody said a word.

It might have been because Allan Sanders was one of the most famous movie stars of the golden age of Hollywood.

Every man in the room, with the possible exception of Hemingway, had grown up watching Sanders' athletic form of swashbuckling dramatics. Irish-born, his family had immigrated to Canada when he was only a child. He had moved to California in his mid-twenties and had played some of the most manly roles in movie history — characters like John Paul Jones in *Bonhomme Richard,* Elliot Ness in *The Chicago Story,* and Alvin York in *Lone Hero.* Because of a bum knee he'd acquired in a fall while filming a sword fight in *The Knight of Sherwood,* he'd been listed as 4-F during the second great war, but he'd done his part anyway, portraying a string of daring soldiers in Hollywood war epics designed to boost the sale of War Bonds.

His on-screen heroics were only one part of the Allan Sanders legend. His off-screen life had been almost as adventurous. He had smuggled arms to the IRA during the roaring twenties, fought shoulder-to-shoulder with Basque nationalists during the Spanish Civil War — barely surviving the horrendous bombing of Guernica — and had made midnight marine bootlegging runs between Nova Scotia and Boston during Prohibition. He had captured the imagination of thousands of teenage boys by bedding the most desirable women in Hollywood. One actress, handpicked by a celluloid king for a meteoric film career, spent a long weekend in Tahoe with Sanders and was never the same again. The Hollywood magnate vowed revenge, purchased Sanders' contract, and forced him to do a series of villain roles designed to make him the most hated man in the movies. Something about Sanders' boyish charm bled through, though, and audiences loved him more.

Plainly put, Allan Sanders was a motion-picture god. Seeing him standing in Hemingway's parlor should have been enough to shock us into silence.

There was more, however. The man who

stood in our midst, half a head taller than anyone else in the room, looked like a walking train wreck. Time and tide had taken their toll. The great actor's cheeks were blue with a day's worth of beard and intractable dissolution, the result of too many years of drinking, fighting, and whoring in every city that would allow him to light for more than a day or two. He wore a stained pullover shirt and summer wool trousers going threadbare in spots. No shoes or socks. His eyes were bloodshot. His hair hung in near-waxy ringlets. His aroma was as legendary as his screen career.

"We're fucked," Braga said.

Hemingway started pouring coffee into Sanders, who slowly showed signs of attaining complete consciousness.

"He was sent here by the Scripps-Howard papers," Hemingway explained. "Something about covering the revolution. Got mixed up with Castro and his boys down south. He's in good with the rebels, from what he says, so he shouldn't have any problems getting back into the country after delivering the goods."

"All I want to know is whether he can pilot a boat," Braga said.

"The man's a master sailor," Hemingway replied. "Served in the merchant marine as a lad. Has his own schooner, a two-mast job. Over a hundred feet long. A real beauty. Calls it the *Xanadu.*"

"It's here in Cuba?" Rico asked.

"No. It's moored in Monaco. You can take *Pilar.* Better idea in any case. It will cross the strait much more quickly than *Xanadu* ever could. Sanders! You sober yet?"

"Shut up, you old goat," Sanders groaned from the kitchen.

Marisol grasped my arm, seeking reassurance.

"He's okay for the trip?" I asked.

"Sanders? He's been on a tear for thirty years. Liver's probably shriveled up to the size of a prune, but he's seaworthy. I'll guarantee it."

We squeezed six people into the Packard, then skirted the east side of the city to reach the Calle Real, which terminated at Cojimar and the marina. While we didn't see much of the central part of Havana, it was clear from the packed highways and the desperation on people's faces that the reality of the revolution had sunk in.

Braga stopped in a shelled parking lot in the shadow of the sixteenth-century fort next to the marina. I helped Marisol and Lila out of the backseat, while Rico and

Sanders grabbed suitcases from the trunk. Somehow, I noted, Braga had even managed to reacquire my luggage from Colonel Machado — or perhaps I had Hector to thank for that.

The marina was deserted, save for a few fishing vessels and four or five lonely sailboats. There were also a few charter boats bobbing at their moorings, but otherwise it looked as if the Havana marine set had bugged out.

We hustled down the docks to the *Pilar*'s berth, and made a sort of fire brigade to load the luggage. Then I helped Lila and Marisol onto the boat and scrambled on board behind them. Rico could have fallen in, for all I cared. Sanders climbed to the flying bridge and — using Hemingway's keys — powered up the bilge fans. The last thing we needed was to crank the engine and explode alongside the docks. Braga climbed up with him, presumably to stand watch. It seemed Braga saw everything around him in stark detail.

I settled Lila and Marisol on the benches under the flying bridge, in the shade, and then joined Braga and Sanders topside. Rico took a seat in the fishing chair facing stern and rested his feet on a wooden roller. Hemingway had installed the roller on the transom to help land the larger catches.

Sanders started the single Chrysler engine, which rumbled to life with a satisfying roar and a flood of bubbles and disturbed silt.

"You!" he called to Rico. "Cast off the mooring lines!"

Rico turned and looked over his shoulder at Sanders, partly puzzled, mostly annoyed that he was asked to help launch the boat.

"Remove the lines from the dock," Sanders clarified.

Rico jumped to the dock to unhook the halyards from their mooring points, and then tossed them over the gunwale before scrambling back on deck.

"Should have left him," I said. I wasn't certain Sanders or Braga heard me. Then I caught a glimpse of Braga in my peripheral vision. He looked as if he was smiling. It was the kind of grin George Raft might have given to some stool pigeon, just before shoving him out a tenth-story window.

"Should be smooth sailing," Sanders said. "Sky's clear to the horizon and the water's flat. We should make the Keys before dark."

"You know the way?" I asked.

"Point 'er north and hold compass. She'll get there."

"What about the Cuban patrols? Are they going to be a problem?" Braga asked.

"What patrols? There's a revolution going on. Haven't you heard? Every military man in the country has either deserted or been put on the front lines to be mown down by the rebels. We shouldn't have any problems with the Coast Guard."

"You sound happy about that," I said.

"Don't see as how it makes much difference. Batista raped this country. Castro means well, but one despot is pretty much like another. I've been through this before. Spain, the thirties. Can't say Franco has been any better for the country than Azana was, and I fought for the bastard. The main difference is I get along with Castro. Can't abide Batista."

I watched as he navigated the channels along the Malecòn toward the deep blue water.

"Let me know when you get into open sea," I said.

"Will do, Cap'n."

I clambered down to the main deck and found Marisol sitting next to Lila, her arm around the girl's shoulders. Lila had been crying again. In fact, I had a hard time remembering a five-minute period since picking her up at Hector's plantation when she hadn't been weeping. It was hard, what she saw me doing to her. I placed my hand on Marisol's head.

"It'll be okay," I said. "Don't worry."

Neither Marisol nor Lila acknowledged my words.

I went below, into the cabin, and fished around in the cubbies until I found a set of charts. I took one of them with me back up to the deck. By that time, Sanders had come down from the flying bridge, and was piloting the *Pilar* from the main console at the front of the deck. Rico remained stretched out in the fishing chair, his face turned toward the sun. I showed Sanders the chart, and he nodded when he saw the course I pointed out.

"We are in open water," he announced fifteen minutes later, and then he turned the boat about to port.

Rico must have felt the pressure in his seat, or perhaps he noted that the position of the sunshine on his face had shifted. He jumped from the seat. "What are you doing?" he demanded.

"Changing course," Sanders said. "Cap'n's orders."

"What captain? I thought you were the captain!"

"On this voyage, the man with the gun is the captain."

Rico charged me. Before he could get

within five feet, I had my Colt out and at my side. He jerked to a halt under the flying bridge.

"Mac! What are you doing?"

"The right thing," I said. "Mr. Sanders, set a course for Georgetown."

"Georgetown?" Rico said. "Where the fuck is Georgetown?"

"Grand Cayman," Sanders said. "Where the cap'n wants to go."

"No!" Rico yelled. "You can't! I won't let you!"

Before I could stop him, he grabbed Lila and dragged her toward the stern transom. I started to dash after him — after all, where could he go? — when he pulled a small revolver from his jacket pocket and pressed it to Lila's temple. She wailed and thrashed, but couldn't break free from Rico's viselike grasp.

"Rico! Stop!" Marisol screamed. "Don't be foolish."

"We are going to *Miami!*" Rico snarled. "My money is waiting for me there, and we are taking the girl to her father. You will not cheat me out of what I am due."

"Due?" I said. "For what? Killing Gopaldo? Killing McCarl? You think you've earned this reward as some kind of blood money? Cecil Hacker is a pervert. I'm not turning Lila over to him and neither are you."

Lila's fearful features transformed to rage. "You killed Danny?" she cried, as she tried to turn her face to Rico, ignoring the revolver's barrel pressed against her skull.

"He did," Marisol said. "I heard him confess it to Hector last night. Your friend was going to take you to Grand Cayman himself, because he did not trust Rico."

"Smart man," I said.

"Rico told Hector he got your friend drunk and then shot him as they walked down the street," Marisol said.

"You *bastard!*" Lila said, her adolescent brain unable to process the fatal stakes she was playing. "I'll kill you!"

She reached up and tried to claw at Rico's face, but he slid his hand up, snared her hair, and yanked her head backward. She screamed and fell to her knees. I yanked my Colt up and drew a bead on him, but Rico shifted the gun from her temple to the top of her head, aiming straight down.

"Don't try it, Mac!" he said. "I'll kill her. I swear it! Turn this boat around and make course for Miami. I will not be denied —"

A whipcracking sound echoed from above my head, and a scarlet floret appeared in the center of Rico's throat. He let go of Lila, who crumpled to the deck, and reached up to touch the wound, as if unable to believe it existed. The spot turned into a spreading blotch of red, and a confused expression crossed Rico's features. He made a liquid gargling sound, looked over my head, and raised the revolver.

Braga fired again from the flying bridge, catching Rico in the middle of the chest. It should have dropped him, but instead he spun halfway to his left. By then he must have been running on fumes, but he made one more attempt to raise the gun. Braga's next shot caught him at the bridge of the nose, snapping his head back. The momentum carried him backward to the transom, and his own weight pivoted him around the roller Hemingway had installed and into the brine on the other side.

"High damned time," Sanders exclaimed, "that boy made me nervous."

"Must be getting rusty," Braga said. "Time was, I'd have only needed one shot."

Lila had curled up into a fetal ball near the fishing chair. Marisol rushed to her side and cradled her on the blood-spattered deck, rocking her back and forth.

I swung around from under the flying bridge and pointed the Colt at Braga. By then he'd already holstered his own pistol and was heading for the ladder.

"Whoa, cowboy," he said, his hands in the air. "Cool your jets. You're safe. I was only under orders to take out Rico."

"Whose orders?"

Braga descended the ladder then waggled a finger at me as he hit the deck. "There are things you need to know and things you don't need to know," he said. "I'll let you figure out which one this is. How far is it to Georgetown? I could use a drink."

Sanders said, "Join the club, mate."

I didn't waste time trying to figure out who had ordered Braga to take out Rico. I'd noted how chummy Braga had become with Hector, and I thought maybe Hector found a way to cleanse the bloodstains Rico had spilled on the Gonzalez family honor.

Chapter Thirty-One

We anchored at Georgetown the next morning. It took me about three hours to locate Lila's stepfather. A good night's sleep had calmed her considerably, given the trauma she'd undergone the day before, and when I delivered her to her stepfather's house she fell into his arms, sobbing with relief and joy. I didn't ask for a reward, but he forced a nice fat check on me anyway. I have come to appreciate the gratitude of wealthy people.

I needn't have worried about Cecil "The Madman" Hacker's wrath. By the time I got back to Miami, the newspapers were full of how he'd taken his fishing boat out into the Gulf Stream and never returned. They made it out to be a simple accident on the high seas, but the undertone in the stories made it plain the Trafficante organization had assured they wouldn't suffer any blowback from Hacker's Treasury Department indictment. I found it ironic that both Hacker and Rico seemed to have suffered similar fates.

I have no idea what happened to the money Hacker had put in the bank for Rico. It's probably still there, waiting.

A few bits of news leaked out of Cuba over the next year, and I learned some things from people who joined the flood of refugees who traversed the Florida Straits to escape Castro's post-revolutionary bloodbath.

Batista was out of the country before I even set foot on the *Pilar.* He island-hopped over to the Dominican Republic, along with a king's ransom in stolen money, and bounced around a succession of semi-friendly countries before finally lighting in Portugal, where he lived for the rest of his miserable life.

The same couldn't be said for his loyal associates, many of whom stayed behind to try to stave off the inevitable takeover by Castro and Che. They were mown down like the stubble in Hector's sugarcane fields. Hector didn't contact me, and after a while he became nothing more than a noble memory. I never received substantiated confirmation, but I have a feeling Hector ended his days with his back against the bullet-pocked wall of La Cabana fortress.

As did Jaime Guzman, I'm sad to say. That execution was documented all too graphically on film. Castro had a major bug up his ass about police officers who had served under Batista, whether they had been good cops or corrupt ones. Despite Jaime being one of the good guys with a heart the size of all Havana, he was swept up in the terror that followed the insurrection. The pictures show he met death bravely, refused the blindfold, and stared down the firing squad with an expression that could only be described as steely.

Allan Sanders returned to Havana without a hitch. He hung out with his buddies Castro and Che for a few months, and even made a completely awful movie about the revolution. I saw part of it in a steamy theater in Miami, but walked out before the third reel. Sanders ran out of money and had to sell his possessions to make ends meet. With nothing to keep him stateside, he retreated to Monaco and lived on his schooner *Xanadu* for a few months while trying to forge a new career in European cinema. He got a minor role in an Italian art film, but otherwise the stars aligned no better for him there, and eventually he was forced to part with the last love of his life. He found a buyer for *Xanadu,* and set out on one final transatlantic voyage to deliver the boat to its new owner in Nova Scotia.

He never made it. Somewhere between the Mediterranean and the Bay of Fundy, *Xanadu* disappeared. Some people think Sanders found a cozy sheltered port on a remote North Sea island and then drank himself to death. Others thought he'd fallen prey to a rogue wave in the remnants of a hurricane. Almost everyone figured he was dead. He vanished only a few months past his fiftieth birthday, and the mystery surrounding his end only enhanced his Hollywood legend.

As he had predicted, Hemingway took Castro sail fishing on the *Pilar* several months after the revolution. A couple of years later Hemingway swallowed the loud end of his double-barreled twelve gauge in Ketcham, Idaho. I was saddened by his passing, although I thought any sane person could see it coming from a mile away. To be perfectly honest, I was surprised he lasted as long as he did.

I heard from Braga a few years after we fled Havana. He was in New Orleans, establishing a beachhead for the mob out of the back of a restaurant on the Rue Charles. Apparently Trafficante had liked Braga's work in Cuba and decided he could handle some added responsibility.

Marisol and I went hot and heavy for a while. She moved into my house and made a game stab at playing the American domestic housewife role, even though she refused to make it official with a ring and a preacher. She was Catholic, after all, and — as far as she knew — still married to Hector. She wasn't about to add bigamy to her laundry list of sins.

Then, in late 1959, we received a letter from a Key Biscayne attorney. Somehow, Hector had managed to set up a trust fund for Marisol through a Cayman bank, to assure that her transition to America would be as painless as possible. He must have thought her culture shock would be traumatic because the size of the fund made for major general anesthesia.

The money became a ditch between us that grew into a creek and then a river and, finally, an ocean. At some level I had always known I was playing second fiddle to her rabid nationalism. Now that she had the resources, she became active in the anti-Castro movement. Over the course of a few months she grew more distant and eventually disappeared entirely into the embrace of the community of Cuban refugees in the burgeoning Little Havana section of Miami.

I came home one day and her closet was empty, her bags missing. There was a note on the kitchen table. I didn't read it. Didn't need to. I knew where she had gone and why. I had lost her to Cuba. Deep down, I had known I would, eventually.

I saw her from time to time, mostly at rallies or benefits to raise funds for Cuban freedom fighters. Sometime around the Bay of Pigs she became part of a group of Havana expats who infiltrated back into Cuba to join the underground resistance against Castro. Most of those efforts were doomed from the outset. I never heard from her again. I don't like to think about what must have happened. I hope it was quick and painless.

I used Hacker's money to buy the Buick Roadmaster.

Someone stole it from the front of my office three months later.

I never recovered it. The insurance bought me another car, but this time I went for something a little less flashy and less attractive to thieves.

In short, I lost all the spoils of my final Havana adventure. It seemed appropriate somehow. Cuba had never been a lucky place for me. I couldn't think of any reason why my last trip there should have ended any differently.

I'm still on the job. Mostly I tail errant spouses and insurance frauds, and sometimes I take on a missing-person case. I've found a few runaways over the last year or so. I return them to their parents and most of them last about a week before bolting again. That's fine with me. I like to think of it as job security.

I still have dreams at night, but they're not always about the boy on the breaking ice. Sometimes I dream about Havana. In my dreams, I'm standing on the tenth-floor balcony of a hotel on the Prado, gazing over the Malecòn at the billion pinpoints of reflected sunlight on the whitecaps of the Caribbean. It's morning, before the heat has sucked the life out of the city, and the cool breeze off the salt washes over my face and chest like a granted wish. Marisol is by my side, under my protective arm, and we stand and stare at the water, unable to pull ourselves away from the beauty that is eternal and unmolested by human ambition and political greed.

It's a nice dream. I go to bed each night with a prayer to whichever deity will take my call that I'll have it just one more time.

ABOUT THE AUTHOR

After retiring from a quarter-century career as a forensic psychologist, **Richard Helms** now teaches psychology at a North Carolina college. He has been nominated three times for the Shamus Award, four times for the Derringer Award, and once each for the Macavity Award and the Thriller Award. He is the only author ever to win the Derringer Award in two different categories in the same year (2008), and he won the Thriller Award for Best Short Story in 2011. *The Mojito Coast* is his sixteenth novel. A past board member of Mystery Writers of America, Richard Helms lives with his lovely wife Elaine in a small town in North Carolina.